TOOTH, CLAW, AND VENOM

DELIA CORTEZ

An imprint of Diogenes Club Press

Worldly, Whimsical, and Weird Books

www.diogenesclubpress.com

Dallas, TX

DC Dreams, an imprint of Diogenes Club Press
8619 Reva St. Dallas, TX 74227
www.diogenesclubpress.com

ISBN: 9781622010097
Library of Congress Control Number: 2017955896

 PROLOGUE

Bronwyn Liddle gasped for breath.

"Pull the laces tighter, Jenna," Alys Sayer ordered the young handmaiden.

"They will not go any tighter," Bronwyn grunted. She felt Jenna's boot in the small of her back. She flailed her arms wildly at her sides as the servant girl yanked on the corset laces.

"If you can still complain, your waist is not small enough."

"If my face begins to turn purple, please resuscitate me."

Alys rolled her eyes. "Do not be so dramatic."

"How am I supposed to dance if I cannot even breathe?"

"And whom do you expect will ask you to dance?"

"I will have you know, there are plenty of men who ask me to dance."

"They will now, anyway." Alys flicked her fingers at Jenna to dismiss the young maid from the room. She rose to turn her best friend towards the tall, gilded mirror in the center of the enormous dressing chamber. "There. You see? You look quite lovely."

Bronwyn smoothed her hands down the sides of the silky emerald green gown. Her waist looked small enough for a man to encircle with his hands. The swell of her full, ivory pale breasts rose and fell over the suggestive décolletage. She tossed her head, and the long, loose dark auburn curls from her elegant twist brushed teasingly over her cleavage.

Her mouth curved into a small, satisfied smile. Alys was the favorite amongst their male acquaintances with her sweet, patrician face, brilliant blue eyes, honey blonde hair and slender figure, but Bronwyn was not without her own admirers. At twenty-seven, passed the full blush of their youth, the two friends were still regarded as very beautiful, even in the most fashionable society.

"Mrs. Devereaux assures me her party promises to be the greatest social event of the year," Alys said, sitting at Bronwyn's brass vanity to twist her long, sleek hair into a careful braid around the crown of her head.

Bronwyn sat carefully upon a stool and folded her hands primly in her lap. She smirked. "Mrs. Devereaux always believes her parties are the greatest social events of the year. She is nearly always quite mistaken."

Alys' blue eyes twinkled. "I heard from Lady Courtney that a Spanish Count arrived in town a couple days ago and has taken up residence in Regent's Park next door to Lord and Lady Bailey. Of course, you know how the Lady is. She paid a call on him right away."

"What is he like?"

Alys shook her head. "I don't know. Lady Bailey has been most mysterious about him. He was indisposed when she attempted to call, so she left a card with his man."

"He hasn't returned their hospitality? That's quite rude, isn't it?"

"Well, the Spanish have different ways than us, but I understand he did return the visit that evening. Lady Courtney assures us the Lady Bailey invited him to the ball at the Devereaux estate tonight."

Bronwyn lifted her eyebrows. "Does she expect he will attend?"

Alys smiled. Her eyes drifted away, as though she were envisioning the Spaniard. Despite her many admirers, Alys had never been attached to any man. None of them ever seemed to hold her interest for very long. New gentleman always piqued her curiosity. "I certainly hope so. I would love to meet a foreign count. Lady Bailey seemed to think she had persuaded him."

"Are you thinking of throwing yourself in his path?"

Alys lifted her shoulders delicately. "Well, I do not know, do I? I haven't even seen him yet. A Spanish count...he sounds much more exciting than the endless parade of Baronets, Marquis and Earls who expect me to swoon over their titles."

"Not to mention the untitled gentleman who expect their money to turn your head?"

"Don't be snide, Wyn. You know Father would never allow me to marry below my station. He expects me to marry up."

"Yes, well, I suspect the King himself would fail to meet your father's standards."

Alys lifted her chin. "He enjoys keeping me near. I cannot blame him. I am quite delightful company."

Bronwyn laughed. "Indeed you are. A Spanish count is no higher than an Earl, you know."

"I don't care about that; you know that. I would refuse the Duke if he were a dreadful bore like most of the nobility." She sighed. "I just want to meet someone interesting. Someone with life and wit and conversation."

"It is difficult when the gentry continue to marry among their cousins and close acquaintances. There is little opportunity to expand the social circle and learn new and exciting things about the world."

"Oh, I would like to see Spain. Barcelona and Madrid…I hear they're worlds like in a fairy tale. The men and woman dance in the streets, and the sun shines so brightly, it's as though the buildings are made of gold."

"I hope the Count is all you hope him to be. I would hate for your pretty fantasies to come to nothing."

Alys tossed her head. "Your sarcasm will not dampen my spirits this evening, Bronwyn Liddle."

She laughed. "It never does."

* * *

Alys spoke in low tones to the young, handsome man bending over her hand at the small, candlelit table on the edge of the Devereaux's grand dance floor. Bronwyn did not need to hear Alys' words to surmise their context. The young man stepped away with a disappointed expression she had seen enough times. "Another casualty of your razor tongue?" Bronwyn teased when the young man had disappeared into the crowd of coiffed and bejeweled dancers and guests.

"I told him I was feeling faint," Alys explained, fluttering her fan on her breast as though to cool herself.

"He was quite handsome, though."

"Mm. Yes, well, he was about five years younger than us."

"There is nothing wrong with a younger man. I hear they possess assets the older gentlemen do not."

Alys scoffed. "You heard from Lady Courtney. She knows nothing about it. I hear men improve with age. I would prefer a mature and experienced man to an eager youth. Sophistication is far more appealing than keenness."

Bronwyn laughed. "Miss Marietta Kincaid does not seem to feel the same. Do you see with whom she is dancing?"

Alys strained to peer through the crowd at their young, dark-haired friend. She stifled a bark of laughter behind her satin-gloved hand. "Mr. Mallory? The yeoman?"

"Oh, yes. He has been skulking around her all evening. I hear he's even been around the estate most days calling upon her father."

"Indeed? Do you think he intends to make her an offer?"

"Kitty thinks so. She says Marietta seems quite taken with him."

"Scandalous. Does not their father mind he is beneath them?"

"His family is extremely well-off these days. They did very well for themselves. Kitty says her father is struggling since the war."

"Kitty should not be discussing her family's financial situation. Perhaps a common yeoman is the appropriate choice for her sister after all."

"Marietta is a sweet girl, but she is not beautiful, and she is not rich. She should not refuse a man simply because her friends don't approve."

Alys rolled her eyes. "I do detect censure in your tone, Wyn."

"No. You are not wrong. Kitty should not be discussing such matters outside the family."

"If Marietta marries the man, will we be expected to call upon them?"

"Of course we will. She's our friend whether she's married to a gentleman or a yeoman."

Alys sighed. "Well, I will try to get used to the idea."

"I reckon you ought to do. Besides, he is a little handsome, isn't he?"

"If you like that sort of thing."

Bronwyn laughed. She cut off abruptly as a tall, well-built gentleman approached them. Lord Eric was a very handsome man in an elegant black suit and top hat. When he caught their eyes and swept the hat from his head to bow to them from several tables away, his caramel-colored curls shone in the glittering chandelier. He smiled at them, but his dark eyes were for Alys alone.

Alys groaned behind her fan. Despite the Earl's attractive appearance, Alys found the man dreadfully dull. He seemed either not to notice or simply did not regard her deep dislike of him. He never failed to appear at any ball or party Alys attended. "Oh, here he comes," she complained. "If he reaches us, he'll ask me to dance, and I can't keep refusing him each time. It's terrible manners. And if I manage to avoid him asking, he'll talk my ears off about his properties all night long."

Bronwyn smirked. "Go. I will make up a tale."

Alys wasted no time. She feigned a swoon. Bronwyn covered her mouth with her fan to conceal a smile as her friend rose unsteadily to her feet and rushed away from the table without a backward glance.

Lord Eric darted to follow her, but Bronwyn rose to block his way. She smiled at him. He sighed almost imperceptibly and paused to face her. "Good evening, Lord Eric," she said cheerfully.

He bent over her hand compulsorily. "Lady Bronwyn, it is a pleasure to see you as always. But where has the Lady Alys gone? Is she quite well?"

Bronwyn waved a dismissive hand. "She was feeling rather faint. She must have laced her corsets too tight."

Lord Eric looked appalled at this remark. Bronwyn smirked behind her fan. "I see. Well..." He appeared to be considering fleeing from her but seemed to decide it would be very ill treatment indeed. He smiled stiffly. "Are you well, Lady Bronwyn?"

"I am, thank you." She smiled. "Avoiding unwanted attention from a number of the gentleman, as usual."

He smiled as though this were something he knew quite a lot about. "Ah. I understand. There are many cads and dreadful bores at court. It must be difficult for a lady."

Bronwyn lowered her fan to show him her teeth. "It is indeed very difficult."

She didn't think he understood quite as well as he asserted. He droned on for the next several minutes about his newest horse, a sturdy, dapple grey mare with long, black hair. She stared at him blankly, hoping he wouldn't mistake her glazed expression for amiable interest. "I think Lady Alys would love her. She's quite a gentle ride, despite her enormity."

"Oh, I don't think Alys likes horses. She much prefers walking to riding, I'm sure."

He looked so crestfallen, she almost felt guilty. She forgot him seconds later as surely as though he'd never been there at all. Bronwyn's breath caught in her throat as she caught sight of the man approaching them. He was tall and dark, and his suit was the finest in the ballroom. He did not wear a hat, and his black, shoulder-length hair brushed his broad shoulders. His skin was a shade darker than Lord Eric's, despite the Earl's summer tan. He must be the Spanish Count. She felt a rush of heat to her belly as she met his dark, flashing gaze.

There was something very ominous in the air around him. His smile seemed to conceal something mysterious and deadly. A shiver raced down her spine. She ignored it. He paused in front of her and offered his hand. When she took it, he bowed and kissed her knuckles. The very tip of his hot, wet tongue darted out as though to sample the taste of her skin. She exhaled in a tiny, inaudible sigh.

"My lady, I apologize for keeping you waiting." His accent was musical, as though he was playing with the English words. "I believe I promised you this dance."

Her pulse leapt. His long, slender fingers were cold, and her body heated up as though to warm them. She inclined her head, but she did not open her mouth to speak to him as he led her towards the dance floor. He pulled her close against his lean body. His dark, almond shaped eyes burned down into hers.

He leaned down to speak in her ear. She was grateful his hands were cool. Fire spread from the places he touched her straight down to her core. Her cheeks flushed. "I am Lord Rafael, Count of Toreno." His breath tickled the bare skin of her neck and shoulders.

She smiled and leaned back to look up into his eyes. "I have heard you were in town."

"Word spreads quickly here."

"Yes, indeed it does. There are many silly people who have little better to do than report on all the comings and goings in Regent's Park."

He laughed. It was a low and husky sound. It vibrated from his throat and spread across every inch of her. Every move and sound he made seemed to resonate deep inside her body and settle into the heat and moisture between her legs. Her lips parted involuntarily. Her tongue flicked across her teeth as she watched his full, sensual mouth form the words. "And what is your name?"

It took her a moment to realize he'd asked her a question. Her eyes flicked back up to his. "Lady Bronwyn Liddle."

"Bronwyn," he repeated. It sounded strange and sensual when he said it. "A strong, beautiful name for a beautiful woman."

She laughed. "I heard you Spaniards are charming."

He lifted an eyebrow. "Am I charming you?"

She smiled. She felt his hand move against her back as if to explore the contours of her body. She lifted her chin. "Yes."

She was mortified. She didn't know why she'd said this, but she felt so hot and strange, as though every sense in her body had been awakened and focused upon a single point in the universe. She could smell him as strongly as if his bare flesh was pressed against hers. She couldn't identify the scent, but it sent curls of arousal coursing through her.

She blinked and shook her head slightly as if to clear it. "I'm sorry. That was very bold."

"I like bold women. A woman who is too afraid to share her emotions is hardly living at all." He dipped his head to murmur in her ear. "Are you living?"

Her voice was breathless. "Yes."

"Are you really?"

She glanced into his breathtaking face. He had high cheekbones, and his tanned skin looked so smooth she was sure it would feel like silk beneath her fingers. The world seemed to blur and slow around them. His eyes were so alive, so intense and consuming she wondered how the other guests and dancers had ever seemed anything more than paper dolls or children's toys. No. She had never lived before, not until she looked into his eyes. "No."

He smiled. His hand tightened on the small of her back. His mouth brushed the delicate skin between her neck and shoulders. His breath was like liquid ice but she felt a thrill jolt through her entire body. "I can make you feel so alive," he murmured against her skin.

A slow delicate burn pulsed between her legs. "Your skin is so cold."

"Yours is so hot. Bronwyn. I can make you feel things you've never felt."

She was sure the proper ladies and gentleman of the English gentry were astonished by this scandalous display. She did not care. She felt suddenly reckless and aroused. The rest of the world might have stopped around them. She sighed heavily.

"Do you want me to make you feel?"

"Yes." She hadn't even realized she'd spoken it aloud. He smiled. She blinked and shook her head as if to clear it. Her cheeks flushed.

"You run so hot."

"Why is your skin so cold? It's as cold as death."

He smiled. "I am more alive than you could possibly imagine. I could show you everything. I could show you the world."

The music stopped. Bronwyn blinked and joined the other dancers as they clapped politely. She felt as though the dance had only just begun. She took a step back from him and curtsied. "Thank you for the dance, Lord Rafael."

He smiled and inclined his head. When she turned away, he caught her arm and drew her against him. She gasped. She could feel his stiff cock pulsating against the small of her back. He flattened his palm against her belly. "Remember what I said." His voice was a purr and it spread through her body like wildfire. "I could make you feel so alive."

She caught her breath and tore away from him. She did not turn back to look at him over her shoulder. Her cheeks burned. She lifted her chin and ignored the stares of her acquaintances and fellow guests.

Alys met her halfway to their table. Her blue eyes were narrow. "What was going on with that man, Wyn?"

"He's Lord Rafael," Bronwyn replied vaguely.

"Yes, I understand that. And you were making an absolute spectacle of yourself with him!"

Bronwyn's cheeks felt as though they might burst into flame. "Perhaps I drank too much wine."

"Perhaps." Alys frowned at her in disapproval. She caught Bronwyn's elbow and dragged her towards the table. "Everyone will be talking about it now. They will say all sorts of things about your character and your breeding."

Bronwyn rolled her eyes. "Let them talk. I don't care what any of them think of me, anyway. They're silly."

Alys sighed. "Yes, I know, but they are our friends and acquaintances. It's our society."

"What do I care about society?"

Alys shook her head. "Wyn, you cannot behave like a wanton rebel forever. You will have to settle down and marry some day. Do not destroy your reputation before you even get the chance."

Bronwyn rolled her eyes, but she did not have a response to this. Alys was not wrong.

Her friend's eyes drifted over her shoulder. Her expression changed dramatically. There was a wistful, dreamy quality to her gaze. "He is gorgeous, isn't he?"

Bronwyn did not turn to glance over her shoulder. She could feel his gaze as surely as she still felt his hands on her body and the hot moisture between her legs. "He is something more than that," she said. "He is some sort of beast."

Alys laughed. Across the ballroom, Lord Rafael winked and flicked his tongue across his upper lip for a split second. She pressed her hands to her cheeks. "I want to meet him."

Bronwyn lifted an eyebrow. "Aren't you worried about your reputation?"

"Yes," Alys admitted. "But there's something about him, isn't there?"

"Yes, there is. I'm not sure it's quite right."

* * *

A light, gentle breeze fluttered the sheer curtains over her open window. Her skin felt hot and charged despite the coolness of the night. She kicked her heavy blankets from her legs. Her skin quivered in the chill breeze. The heat was inside her. The cooling air was like a soothing caress. Her muslin nightgown dragged across her nipples. They tautened, and she exhaled heavily, pushing her hand down into the folds of fabric between her legs.

He was above her before she'd noticed the air had shifted. His body was cold and heavy atop hers. She looked up into his eyes. She didn't scream or struggle or ask how he'd gotten inside her private chamber in the dead of night. He did not speak to her or explain his presence there. He dipped his head. His mouth slanted over hers. His tongue forced past her lips to stroke insistently against hers. She felt his teeth nip at her lower lip. She tasted her own blood.

He reached between them, and she felt the thin, delicate fabric of her nightgown fall away from her body as he tore it in a single, effortless motion. The chill of his firm, rippled flesh sent a shiver through her entire body. He brushed his fingers across the sensitive tips of her breasts. She trembled and moaned low in her throat. She moved restlessly against him.

His long, black hair tickled her skin as he bent his head to rake his tongue across her nipple. She jolted and clutched at his head to hold him to her. He caught her wrists and pinned them down at her side. He sucked her nipple into his mouth, rolling it with his tongue. She moaned and pushed against his ice cold hold. He ignored her struggles. His fingers bit into her wrists and his tongue stroked and swirled across her nipple until she thought she might come undone. His thick, hard cock throbbed against her inner thigh. She ached desperately for him.

She moaned his name. His sensual mouth curved as he lifted his head to peer

11

into her eyes once more. He bared his teeth in a sharp, dangerous smile. He bent his head to kiss her neck. He opened his mouth against her flesh, and even his breath was cold and moist.

His tongue flicked over her neck, tasting the delicate sheen of salt on her skin. Her hands tightened convulsively. She arched up into him. He nudged her legs apart with his knee. She did not notice when he released her wrists to reach down between them.

He entered her in a swift motion, and his teeth sank into the soft flesh between her neck and shoulders. She cried out. Sharp pain jolted through her where his teeth pierced her skin and he thrust forcefully inside her slick, aching depths. His cock was long and wide, and it filled her quim as though she had been made for him. She'd been a virgin moments before. She felt a strange, almost pleasurable tearing inside as he burst roughly through her maidenhead. Her muscles clenched, and she gritted her teeth against the searing pain.

He moaned low in his throat as her muscles convulsed around him. He sucked hard on the wound in her neck. Blood spilled from his lips and ran in rivulets into her hair and across her pillow. Her body rocked with the force of his frenzied thrusts. His hands stroked roughly up and down her body. He clutched her hips, tilting them up push more deeply inside her. He kneaded her breasts with the other hand, teasing the nipples between his fingertips.

She threw her head back and moaned as a wave of pleasure crashed over her body. Her muscles tightened and quivered. His teeth scraped her delicate, sensitive skin. Vaguely, she caught the scent of roses and blood and something oddly, intensely familiar. It was a smell she knew, but it wasn't her smell.

He clutched the sides of her face in his hands as his thrusts grew swifter and more frantic. She no longer felt his teeth, but his mouth was fused to her neck as though he were sucking the last of her life from her veins. She felt as though she might float away on a cloud of pleasure. She wondered if she was dying. Her eyes felt heavy. She did not resist the force of his body as it pounded up inside her so she thought she could surely not contain him any longer.

He let out a low, feral growl from low in his throat, and his fingers clenched on her hips as he exploded in climax. His seed pumped inside her. It was as cold as the trail of spit he left across her neck.

He collapsed atop her, but he did not gasp for breath. He lay perfectly, deathly still. Then he lifted his head. His mouth was smeared with thick, scarlet blood. Her moan was barely audible. Her eyes drooped, and then they closed.

* * *

Bronwyn jolted awake. She felt hot and feverish. A thick sheen of sweat beaded on her forehead. She gasped for breath. She could still feel the sensation of Rafael's cock pumping inside her. Her breasts felt charged and sensitive as though a single touch would tilt her back into the vague fog of intense, painful pleasure.

She groped frantically at her body. She was dressed. Her blue silk nightgown was not lying in tatters by her bedside. It hadn't been real. Rafael had not come to her in the night. Her body still quivered from the intensity of the sensations, but they had not been real. She reached under her gown and encountered the searing moisture between her legs. She moaned as the memory of the dream coursed through her once more. She reached instinctively for her neck. There was no pain. The skin was smooth and unbroken.

She dropped back down against the pillows. Just a dream. But had it been a dream? It had felt so real, so powerful. She sighed deeply. She closed her eyes and drew a finger across the delicate, electric skin between her neck and her shoulders. She shivered, but she did not slip back into the erotic dream, into the place he had been. She slept, but there was only darkness, and if she dreamt, her dreams were not made flesh.

* * *

Bronwyn awoke with the dawn. The soft rays of sun through the sheer curtains seemed to burn as they fell across her bare arms. She threw aside the heavy blanket and swung her legs over the side of the large, four poster bed. It had only been her imagination. The sun was warm and soft on her ivory skin.

She still felt strange and shaky. When she landed on the soft, thick carpet, her legs wobbled slightly. She padded to the washroom to splash cold water on her flushed cheeks. She could not chase last night's erotic dream from her mind. She did not try. She pictured Lord Rafael above her, his mouth and tongue suckling teasingly on her nipples, his cock stroking inside her until the tension built up and exploded in a tidal wave of shattering sensation. A tender ache thrilled through her quim. She moaned softly under her breath.

She dipped her fingers down to touch the throbbing nub between her legs. It pulsed and quivered. She exhaled heavily. She needed a cold dip in the porcelain tub. Her cheeks flushed as she considered calling Jenna to assist her. Mortification thrilled through her. This was no way for a lady to behave, dreaming of foreign counts and fondling herself like a common street walker.

She settled for splashing the jug of ice cold drinking water across her breasts and between her legs. She gasped from the shock of the chill. It soothed her slightly, and she felt her skin begin to cool to normal. She tugged the bell pull to bring her hand maiden.

Jenna was prompt. "My lady?" She looked surprised to see her lady up so early. "Are you feeling feverish?"

"A bit. Will you bring some cool water for my bath?"

Jenna dipped her head in a bow. "Yes, ma'am. Of course. Right away, but perhaps you should lie down if you are feeling ill."

Bronwyn waved her hand. "I'll be fine. Thank you, Jenna. Just the water, if you please."

She sighed and leaned back against the cold side of the empty porcelain tub. She closed her eyes. She brushed a hand across her pert nipples. A jolt shot through her. She pressed her hands to her sides and squeezed her legs together as though it would cause the tender throb to abate. It didn't.

Her brow furrowed. Blood. She'd nearly forgotten it in the afterglow of the intense sexual release. In her dream, he'd bitten her. She remembered the pierce of his teeth in her tender flesh, the sensation of her life force draining from her in the rush of release. Two deaths: one painful and one so intensely pleasurable. She pictured his mouth smeared with her blood.

She jumped and let out a shriek as Jenna dumped the bucket of cold water over her body. Her eyes flew open, and she sat up, glaring at her hand maiden. Jenna looked sheepish, but there was a glint of satisfaction in her eyes. "I'm sorry, ma'am!" she squeaked. "You looked so feverish."

Bronwyn spluttered, but the cold water had chased the vestiges of arousal from her loins and cooled her hot skin. "A little warning next time, Jenna?"

Jenna dipped in a bow and backed out of the washroom. "Of course ma'am. Sorry, ma'am."

Bronwyn flicked her fingers in dismissal and slid down into the cool water. She sighed softly. It was so cold, goose bumps stood out on her arms and legs and spread across her flat, ivory pale stomach. She kept her hands pinned at her sides. The throb slowly faded to a dull ache.

She climbed out of the chilly bath several moments later. She did not feel clean, though she had scrubbed her skin until it felt raw. She did not call Jenna back to assist her to dress, though she lingered over her toilette. As she did, she considered telling Alys about the dream. Color flooded her cheeks. No. She did not think she could tell anyone of the dream. There were things she needn't share with Alys, no matter how dear she was.

Her father had either not awakened or had gone immediately to his study to conduct business when she'd finally dressed and descended the stairs of the large manor house. She did not peek her head into the study or move towards his chambers to rouse him. Even was she to discover him awake, he would not join her for breakfast. He usually took his meals in his chambers. Bronwyn preferred to eat alone or with Alys, who was usually up at an ungodly early hour.

Bronwyn left the house and strode quickly along the path between her father's and the Sayer's estates. The houses were close together, and the lawns were not large, but they were well-tended by the same gardener, Alec, a sturdy, middle-aged man whose family had been looking after the Liddles for generations. He was probably up and about the grounds somewhere. Her eyes darted from side to side as she took the narrow footpath through the trees and rosebushes towards Alys' house. If she was perfectly honest, she was not looking for Alec.

She half expected, half hoped to receive a call from Lord Rafael that day after their dance, after the thrilling words he'd spoken in her ear. She had not seen him again at the ball, and she had felt so feverish she'd begged off as early as was polite.

She wanted to see him again so badly, she ached.

After everything he'd said, she'd thought he want to see her again, too. Perhaps he said such things to every woman with whom he danced. Perhaps it had been nothing at all to him. He might even enjoy whipping innocent women into a frenzy of lust and arousal.

She flushed in mortification at the idea. Surely he wasn't some sort of bounder. She admitted she knew nothing more about him than his name, and there was something extremely dangerous about him. Perhaps she'd been lucky to escape him when she had. She sighed deeply as she remembered the coolness of his skin as he held her, the intense sensations and images from her dream. She didn't care if he was dangerous. She wanted him all the same.

Alys did not greet her at the door when she rapped upon the large iron knocker on Sayer Manor's front porch. Alys' young maid, Rebecca, pulled open the heavy door as though she had been expecting Bronwyn. She looked troubled. "Good morning, ma'am. The Lady Alys is still abed."

Bronwyn lifted her eyebrows. "Still abed? But it's nearly eight in the morning."

"Yes, ma'am. She didn't stir this morning at her usual hour. She seems to be feeling ill."

"What's wrong with her?"

"Sorry, ma'am. I don't know. She looks pale, and she's very tired."

"Can I see her?"

Rebecca inclined her head deeply. "I'll see if she can see you."

Bronwyn waited in the large, gilded vestibule. She knew it so well, she did not admire the expensive, tasteful decorations or furniture that recommended the Sayers to the politest of society. An anxious sensation gnawed at her belly.

Something was wrong.

Rebecca returned moments later. She was smiling, but it looked as though she were concealing a grimace. Bronwyn knew she was fond of Alys. "The lady is awake right now. She would like some tea and something to eat."

Bronwyn inclined her head. "Thank you, Rebecca. If you prepare a tray, I will bring it up to her."

"Of course, ma'am."

Bronwyn was not accustomed to carrying things up three flights of stairs, but she balanced the heavy silver tray while Rebecca trailed anxiously behind as though prepared to catch her if she fell. Bronwyn dismissed the young servant girl when she opened Alys' bedroom door. Rebecca bowed and backed away, but Bronwyn sensed she did not wish to leave her sick mistress.

Alys was sitting up in the enormous bed. The counterpane was sapphire blue. It matched the young lady's eyes perfectly, but today it was brilliant against her starkly white skin. Bronwyn gasped and rushed inside to lay the tray on her bedside table.

Alys laughed. "Do I look so bad, Wyn?"

Bronwyn took her friends hand. "No. You just need rest and some tea. Perhaps the ball wore you out."

The pale, blonde-haired woman did not look convinced. "Balls do not generally wear me out, but I am feeling very tired."

Bronwyn prepared their tea and handed Alys a cup. The delicate china clattered softly as her hand shook. She took only a sip before she handed the saucer back to Bronwyn. "Are you feeling very ill?"

Alys sighed and leaned back against the pillows. "I just feel so weak. Like the life has been drained from me." Bronwyn frowned at this and leaned forward to examine the pale, tender flesh on her friend's neck. There were two tiny marks, like the points of a needle. Her heart leapt, but the wounds looked long healed, like very ancient scars. They could not be fresh. "What are you doing?"

Bronwyn sat back and looked at Alys. "Nothing." She frowned as she sipped her tea. "Did you have any dreams last night?"

"I'm--what? No." Alys' pale skin pinked, and her blue eyes slid away as if in embarrassment.

Bronwyn studied her with narrow eyes. "Not about Lord Rafael?"

"No! Of course not." She scowled at her Bronwyn. "I am a lady."

Bronwyn lifted an eyebrow. She'd thought the same of herself, but it hadn't changed what she had experienced last night. Nevertheless, she didn't argue. She leaned over Alys to press a palm to forehead. It felt cold and clammy. Her brow furrowed. "Alys, I think something is wrong."

Alys waved her hand weakly. "I am only ill. I will be all right tomorrow. Rebecca thinks I drank too much wine." She sighed and leaned back against the pillows. Her eyes drooped. "I'm so tired. I just need to sleep it off. I'll be all right in the morning."

Bronwyn sighed. She didn't want to leave Alys' side, but she could do no good here by her bedside. Rebecca was a much more capable nurse. She rose and leaned over Alys to kiss her forehead. "I will come back in the morning, then."

Alys smiled slightly, though her eyes did not open. "We can take a horseback ride. I'll be so much better, I'll come to you before the sun's even fully up."

Bronwyn didn't smile. "Yes. Then we can race around the corral. I owe you a crushing defeat."

Alys did not rise to this, as she might normally have done. She was asleep again. Bronwyn kissed her moist forehead and called Rebecca to her side. The path back to the Liddle estate seemed long and painful. She hoped Alys would be better by tomorrow morning, but worry still gnawed at her. She was afraid Alys might not ever be better at all.

She spent the morning on her window ledge with a sketch book in her lap. She didn't think of Alys, though her friend's pale features flashed in her mind from time to time. She thought of Rafael and the strange, intense sensations of his touch, of the troubling dream. From time to time, her hand smoothed over her neck and down her breasts, but she shook her head fiercely and pressed her forehead to the cool, smooth glass of the large picture window. Below, the courtyard was quiet. No visitors passed below or along the streets.

Her thoughts were tangled and hot all day. She took her meals in her chambers, each time sliding the sketchpad under the cushion beneath her to conceal the scandalous images on page after page: Lord Rafael standing alone on a cliff side, his chest bare and flatly muscled, his long, dark hair loose and falling roguishly over his dark, intense eyes; Rafael posing naked, his thick, erect cock jutting from a patch of dark curls...She hadn't quite captured the expression in his eyes or the contours of his body as she'd seen them in her dream, but he stared eerily back out at her from the sketches as though he could look through his rendering's eyes and sense her longing.

She took a hitching breath and decided to toss the sketches into the first fire of the late evening.

There was a rapping on the front door. She rose to shove the sketchbook under her bed. She paused, considering them a moment. Would the lustful images of him ensure another dream? She wasn't certain whether she wanted that or not. She closed her eyes and thought of him. Was it he downstairs, finally coming to call? She let her mind wander, to picture the rooms of the house as though she might sense him in it somewhere.

She felt suddenly strange. A tendril of heat curled from the top of her head to her toes and back up to the moist cleft between her legs. He was here. She sensed him as surely as she'd felt his member stroke inside her again and again. It was more than a dream. It had to be more than a dream.

She dropped her head back and exhaled in a sigh. Rafael...

She heard her own name in the air. There was no sound, but she felt him answer as though he were waiting for her to come to him, to throw herself upon the ground at his feet and open her legs to him, to offer the moist, glistening heat between her legs to his hard, searing member.

She pressed her hands to her burning cheeks. Her stomach rumbled. She hadn't eaten in several hours. Perhaps her father had invited the Count for dinner. If he had, she certainly could not remain up here in her room. She moved to the washroom to press a cold towel to her cheeks and forehead. It soothed her slightly, but heat still pulsated between her legs.

She heard low male voices in the parlor. It might be rude to intrude upon the conversation, but she could not resist poking her head inside the room. Her father, a tall, still lean man in his mid-fifties, stood beside the mantle, sipping amber liquid from a short glass. He looked as serious as ever, but the gleam in his eyes suggested he was enjoying his guest.

It was Lord Rafael, Count of Toreno. Bronwyn wasn't surprised to see him, but the sight of him sent a jolt from her fingers to her toes. He was dressed as richly as the previous evening, and he seemed to be listening politely to his host describe his newest land acquisition.

Her heart leapt. They both turned to her in the same moment. Lord Rafael rose gracefully to his feet so quickly, she did not see him move. His beautiful face seemed illuminated in the warm candlelight. His full, sensual mouth curved slowly into a smile that seemed to reflect the memory of their imagined night together. His eyes glittered as though he, too, had been there, experiencing the intense sensations. Very slowly, almost imperceptibly, his mouth parted and his tongue snaked out to glide across his upper lip.

She bit her lower lip as she resisted the urge to open her mouth, to drag her tongue across her own suddenly dry lips in response. She did not feel embarrassed by his lustful, knowing gaze. On the contrary, her quim throbbed in hunger. Her father might not have been in the room at all. The air around her was charged and sultry.

Rafael strode forward and bent into a low bow. He caught her hand to kiss the knuckles. He nipped ever softly at them with his teeth. She exhaled heavily. "Lady Bronwyn," he greeted in a low, sensual purr.

"Wyn, dear, you know Lord Rafael?" Lord Aaron Liddle asked indifferently as though he hadn't noticed the exchange between them.

"Yes, father," she replied in a level voice that surprised her. "We met last night at the ball."

Aaron inclined his head. "Very good."

Rafael peered up at her through his dark, thick lashes and smirked. He released her hand and straightened. "Your father and I were discussing business."

"Yes. Rafe is interested in purchasing some property here in England."

Bronwyn blinked. Rafe? Had they grown so informal in mere moments? She turned to Rafael. "Will you be here in England all the time, then?"

He laughed. "Don't sound so disappointed."

"No! No, I....I didn't mean..."

He winked at her. "I am only teasing you, Lady Bronwyn."

Aaron swallowed the contents of his glass and moved towards the door. "Rafe, I'll fetch that paperwork for you."

"Very good. Thank you, Aaron."

When they were alone, he advanced upon her immediately. She gasped as he stood directly above her, radiating a curious chill that seemed to burn straight through her clothes. ""I am most delighted to see you again, Lady Bronwyn." He reached out a long, slender finger, dragging it down her cheek.

"And you, Lord Rafael," she breathed.

"Did you have any interesting dreams last evening?"

She blinked at him in surprise and took half a step backward. He closed the distance between them. "No," she lied.

He smirked as though he didn't believe her. "Oh, really? That is a great shame. I had some very...hot dreams."

Her cheeks burned. "Lady Alys is very unwell this morning," she blurted awkwardly.

He lifted his eyebrows. "Ah. That is a great shame. She is your friend, yes?"

"My best friend. She is pale and sickly."

"That is dreadful. Perhaps she has come down with something." He lifted a single black eyebrow. "And you? How are you feeling?"

She lifted her chin. "Perfectly well, thank you."

He cupped the side of her face in his hand and leaned to speak in her ear. His broad, lean chest barely brushed the taut tips of her breasts. "If you begin to feel a little...restless, you know where to find me."

His hand slid down her cheek, over her bare shoulders and down to her finger. He pressed a small, stiff card into her palm. His tongue flicked out to taste the flesh just below her ear. She shivered.

Aaron strode back into the room. Bronwyn started, but Rafael was across the room now, standing beside the mantle. She blinked in surprise. His eyes glittered at her. She turned and fled from the room. She needed several buckets of cold water. She doubted it would slow her pounding pulse or cool the slow burning inside her.

Everything about him was so terribly alive and so terribly dangerous.

* * *

This time when she awoke, he was already at the foot of her bed. He stood there, his ruddy flesh bathed in pale moonlight through the sheers. He was naked. His torso was lean, flatly muscled. It tapered into a V which drew her eyes down to his long, thick cock It jutted out from the soft, curly black hair surrounding it as though it longed to enter her, to impale and thrust inside her until she came apart in his arms.

He didn't speak to her. He looked at her with that knowing gleam in his eyes, as though he knew that she had imagined the sight of him like this since the night they'd met. Her body tingled and quivered. As though she heard his command in her mind, she tossed the blankets from herself. She opened her legs in anticipation of his body joining with hers.

He did not come to her immediately. He stared at her for several long moments. His eyes were dark and glittering with lust. She sighed and ran a hand over her breast, across her belly and between her legs. She rubbed her thighs together in excitement. Her quim trembled with need. She held her arms out to him. He smiled.

He crawled slowly onto the bed, but he did not come atop her. He caught her foot in his hand, lifting her leg so that her silk gown shivered down to her thighs. He kissed each toe slowly, working his way up to her ankle and over her calf. She whimpered softly in impatience. He ran a hand up her thigh. His fingernails were sharp. They left thin, red trails along the soft, sensitive flesh near her wet heat.

His tongue glided over her leg. She dropped her head back and groaned. He was teasing her, whipping her need to fever pitch. She cried out in frustration as he dragged the flat of his tongue on the inside of her thigh, so close she was sure the warmth of her quim would burn him. She arched up and scooted down the bed toward him.

He chuckled low in his throat and snaked his arms beneath her legs to grip her hips. He tugged her down towards his mouth. She gasped as the chill moisture of his mouth opened on her sensitive clit. He sucked it into his mouth, and she moaned long and low in her throat.

His tongue was nimble, and he seemed not to need to take a breath at all. He buried his face in her soft folds and ticked and suckled until she threw her head back and cried out throatily. He tugged her closer, his hands tightening on her hips to still her bucking hips. When she stopped moving, he drew one hand away

21

from her. She made a small, disappointed noise in the back of her throat.

His long, slender fingers dipped inside her, and she shouted out incoherently. His fingers stroked as he suckled, and tension built in her until she knew it would crash over them both. He caressed his free hand over her belly to her breasts. When he encountered the pert, tingling bud of her right nipple, he pinched it gently, rolling it around with his fingertips. She came with a low, husky shout. Rafael bit down on the flesh of her inner thigh, just below her soaked, pulsating quim.

* * *

She shot up in bed, gasping. Rafael was gone. She tossed the covers aside and yanked her muslin gown to her waist. There were no teeth marks, but when she gingerly prodded the hidden cleft between her legs, she whimpered in anguish. It was wet and swollen.

The orgasm had been very, very real.

Rafael had not.

She threw her legs over the side of the bed and dressed quickly. She felt an odd urgency to check on Alys. She had received no word of her illness worsening that evening, but she was desperate to see her friend. The household was sleeping soundly this early in the morning, and the sun would not rise for a few hours.

She stole silently across the courtyard. She had done it many times before, when she was feeling reckless and rebellious. She had nothing to fear on their families' lands, set back from the thoroughfare and surrounded by tall, white stone walls. Tonight, she felt anxious and afraid. Something very, very strange was going on.

Her heart pounded. From the darkness of the large, lush courtyard, a shadow seemed to emerge. It lengthened across the cobblestone paths between the trees and rosebushes. Bronwyn gasped and paused. It passed directly in front of her. It looked like a man. Her breath caught in her throat. She sprung into motion and raced towards the smallest point, where he must be.

The shadow drew back into itself as if it were shrinking. Then it shifted and lifted up, into the air. She thought she heard the soft, almost inaudible beating of tiny wings. She looked wildly around. She was alone in the courtyard.

She turned from the place the shadow had been and sprinted for Alys' house.

The young maid looked astonished to see her, breathless, on the front porch so early in the morning. "Lady Bronwyn!" she exclaimed. "Are you quite all right?"

"Alys," Bronwyn gasped. "I need to see her."

"Of course, ma'am. Right away." She didn't look as though she wanted to let her inside the house, but she could not turn away her mistress' best friend.

Bronwyn took the steps to her friend's bed chamber two at a time. Rebecca was close on her heels with a worried expression that set Bronwyn's stomach into a nervous roiling. Alys was still asleep when they burst into the room. The commotion did not startle or awaken her. She was so pale, Bronwyn's heart plummeted.

Was she already dead? No. She was breathing, faintly, but her skin was so pale, she looked like a fragile porcelain doll. A tear streaked down Bronwyn's cheek. Something had taken her friend. She did not think she would survive the day.

She pulled up a stool beside Alys' bed and took her hand. She looked up at Rebecca. "I'm going to sit with her."

Rebecca bobbed her head. "Yes, ma'am."

"Her forehead is so cold. Will you bring some warm towels?"

"Of course, ma'am. Right away."

When she was gone, Bronwyn frowned down at her friend. She had the powerful urge to check her inner thigh. Were there marks there? Had something more than illness caused Alys' condition? She remembered Rafael's tongue lapping at her clit, his fingers driving into her until she was shuddering and whimpering with orgasm. The image was still poignant. Fear for her friend had not chased away the abstracted, longing sensation.

She pushed the dream memory away with a sick feeling. There was something more happening here. Somewhere in the back of her mind, she wondered if they hadn't been dreams after all. Had she been experiencing something that was happening to someone else...something that was happening to Alys?

Rebecca returned with a warm, wet towel. Bronwyn used it to mop her friend's clammy forehead, then looked up at the maid. "Rebecca, will you bring up breakfast?"

"Of course, ma'am. Right away. I'll rouse the cook to make some ham and eggs."

"Toast and jam will be fine." Her voice stopped Rebecca at the doorway. "Rebecca?"

"Ma'am?"

"Has anyone come into the house?"

"I beg your pardon, ma'am?"

"Have there been any visitors? Has anyone come into Alys' room?"

"Just you and the master, ma'am. He planned to call for a doctor today if she wasn't better."

Bronwyn frowned. She did not think a doctor could help Alys. She wasn't sure anyone could. "Could anyone come through the window?"

Rebecca was confused by this question. "We're on the second floor."

"I know that." She exhaled heavily. "Have you heard anything strange in here at night?"

The maid looked at Bronwyn as though she had gone mad. "No. Just Lady Alys dreaming."

Her pulse leapt. "Dreaming?"

"Yes. She has been in the throes of fever ma'am. She is in pain."

"Has she been moaning?"

"Yes."

Bronwyn gripped Alys' hand tightly. "Thank you, Rebecca. I would appreciate some breakfast now."

Rebecca bowed and left the room as though she could not get away from the noblewoman fast enough. Perhaps Bronwyn really was mad. Surely there was no such thing as...men who could appear in a second story bedroom and make love to one woman as the other experienced it next door. There were no such things as...monsters.

Bronwyn did not eat the toast and jam Rebecca brought up for her. She sipped her tea absently. Alys did not stir. Her lips looked pinched. They were as white as her skin. Bronwyn took a glass from the bedside table and filled it with water from the jug. She climbed into the bed with her friend, lifting her into a sitting position.

Alys' head lulled. She did not seem to notice Bronwyn at all. She pressed the glass to Alys' lips and tipped it. Alys did not swallow it. She coughed and spluttered. It did not wake her. Bronwyn sighed deeply. She wrapped an arm around Alys' shoulders.

Alys' nightgown fell open to reveal her smooth, rounded breasts. It had been torn down the middle as if by a long, sharp fingernail.

Bronwyn gasped and pushed the covers aside to look at her friend. Alys was naked beneath the ripped gown. Her skin looked pale and shimmering in the earliest rays of the sun. Bronwyn blushed. She and Alys were as close as sisters, and she had seen Alys' body many times while being dressed or bathing. It felt strange now to be witnessing the evidence of illicit lovemaking while her friend slept soundly unaware.

Nevertheless, she glanced up at her friend's sleeping face and then opened her thighs to peer at the flesh between her thick, blonde curls and her left thigh. There were marks there: two tiny puncture wounds that looked as though they'd healed long ago. Bronwyn did not gasp. She had expected to see them.

Someone had done something to Alys. If her dreams were any indication, Alys had begged for it. She would not want others to see the evidence of what she had allowed to befall her. Bronwyn moved to the wardrobe to fetch a freshly laundered muslin gown. She redressed Alys, taking care not to jostle her. Alys seemed not to notice her ministrations at all. She did not stir.

Bronwyn stuffed the torn gown deep into the trash bin in the washroom. She hesitated, peering back at Alys, but she turned from the bed and hurried down the stairs, calling for Rebecca. The maid appeared immediately, as though she had been waiting or feared Bronwyn might stir up the entire house. "Ma'am?"

"Has Lord Rafael been here?"

Rebecca blinked at her in confusion. "Ma'am? I'm sorry."

"He has not visited the house?"

"Not that I am aware, ma'am."

"Has Alys mentioned him?"

Rebecca shook her head. "I don't understand the questions, Lady Bronwyn. I do not know who Lord Rafael is."

Bronwyn sighed and returned to Alys' bedside. She remained by her side through the day, mopping her brow with warm and cold towels as her fever chilled and burned. Alys did not know she was there, praying she would awaken and return to life. She did not. She slept so soundly, Bronwyn checked her wrist and listened to her breath every few minutes to ensure she had not drifted away without warning. The Sayer family doctor visited, but he seemed unable to determine the cause of her illness. Bronwyn dismissed him. He was too perplexed to be of any use to Alys.

At twilight, Bronwyn awoke with a start, lifting her head from Alys' bed. She had fallen asleep. Her heart leapt as she looked up into Alys' pale face. She checked her pulse. Still alive. Night was falling. She wasn't sure what would happen when it did, but she intended to stand guard by Alys.

If someone—or something—intended to swoop in on Alys, she would be there to stop them. She didn't know how to fight a creature who drifted in through a second story window and drained its victim's blood, but she was resolved that nothing would happen to her friend tonight.

Her father did not even respond to the note Rebecca carried across the courtyard to inform him that she would be remaining with Alys. The house was quiet. Bronwyn paced the floor beside Alys' bed. As night deepened, her tension heightened.

There was no sound or movement in the courtyard beneath Alys' window. Her eyes were heavy, but she rested her forehead against the window pane and stared firmly down. If he could reach them, she wanted to see how it was done. She sighed. The breeze through the cracked window was warm and balmy.

She might have drifted to sleep, for she started when she felt the shift in the air beside her. Rafael stood over her, looking down. He was not naked, though her eyes raked him hungrily. His allure was intense.

She dropped her feet to the floor as if to stand and face him, but he moved towards her. He leaned over her, pinning her back against the window seat with his dark, glittering eyes. Rafael cupped the back of her neck in his long, slender hand and bent down to press his mouth against hers. His tongue speared out into her mouth to stroke against hers. He fondled her breast over her gown with a touch so soft, it might have been pure air.

She whimpered in the back of her throat and felt heat lance through her. She lifted her hands to wrap around him, to draw him down to her, but he chuckled softly and drew away. The look he gave her was searing. She dropped her head back in a sigh.

His lips curled into a sensual smile. His voice was like a moth's wing caress over her entire body. "Our time will come soon enough. For now you may sleep."

She did. He laid her gently down upon the window seat and pressed his full mouth to hers. He did not caress her body or stroke her with his tongue. His kiss was sweet and tender and soft. She sighed.

With her eyes closed, she felt his teeth pierce the flesh between her neck and shoulders. There was no pain or rush of arousal. It was a gentle sensation. Peace filled her veins as she felt the blood drain slowly. Her limbs grew heavy and so relaxed, she might have been floating on air. The room around her drifted away, but her senses were filled with him, with the serenity and contentment that seemed to be lifting her up and away.

With a last, quiet sigh, she spiraled into sweet darkness.

* * *

The curtain rustled in the breeze, tickling her nose as it brushed across her face. She started and bolted up. She had fallen asleep, stretched out on the padded window seat in Alys' chambers. Her heart pounded. She pushed the curtain hastily aside.

A long shadow stretched across the courtyard below the window and disappeared.

She jumped off the window seat and raced to Alys' side. Two tiny pink puncture marks stood out on her marble pale throat. She watched in horror as the marks healed and faded before her eyes with supernatural speed, leaving the faintest pink shine like two tiny scars. Bronwyn reared back and touched her own neck in sudden terror, but there was nothing.

She had felt Alys' bite, not her own.

For a moment, she did not move. A vein throbbed in her temple. It was real. Whatever it was, it was real.

She rushed to Alys' side. She threw herself upon the bed beside her friend and cradled her in her arms. "I fell asleep, Alys. I meant to stop it. I'm so sorry." Her voice was barely a murmur. Alys could not hear her. Her friend was silent, pale and still. She was as cold as ice.

Alys was dead.

Bronwyn wailed, but her cries and pleas fell on deaf ears. Alys could not wake up or return to her. Her oldest, dearest and closest friend was gone. She could not come back. She pressed her face into Alys' neck where the monster had pierced her. There was no heat or pulse or sign that he had touched her at all, but Bronwyn knew who was responsible. Alys had been murdered. Bronwyn's tears soaked her friend's waxen cheeks and her long, honey blonde hair.

After several long moments, Bronwyn lifted her head and tugged on the bell pull beside her bed.

* * *

"Lady Bronwyn, you must eat something," Jenna said in a hushed tone, as though she were speaking to a dangerous madman or someone on the verge of death.

Bronwyn did not reply. She did not move from her seat beside the window. She stared down into the courtyard below. She waited for him. He would come. It was her turn. He had promised she would be next.

She waved her hand. "Leave me alone, Jenna." Her voice was low and toneless, as if she had been the one to die, rather than Alys.

"I'm so sorry about Lady Alys."

Bronwyn sighed deeply. She nodded, but she did not turn to face Jenna. She pressed her forehead against the cool glass window pane. "It was a monster."

"Sorry, ma'am?"

"Alys was killed."

"Ma'am, Lady Alys fell ill. The doctor said it was a bad humor. Miss Rebecca told me."

"A bad humor?" Bronwyn chuckled derisively. "That isn't anything. It isn't an illness. Something--someone drained the life from her. It sucked her blood until she died of it."

"Ma'am..." Jenna sounded frightened, as though her mistress was speaking terrible blasphemies.

Bronwyn looked at her suddenly. Her large, dark eyes were wide and half-mad. She lifted her chin haughtily. "I know no one would ever believe me. No one will ever do anything to stop him or make him pay. Alys was my dearest friend. She was my only friend. There is nothing else for me to do here."

"I don't understand, ma'am. Your father--"

"My father would not even notice if I disappeared."

"That isn't true, ma'am! Your father loves you. He is always working to secure your future."

"It was a waste." She spun back to peer out the window. "Leave me." She turned back to look at Jenna. There was nothing in her eyes now, no affection or sorrow. "Thank you for all you've done. You've been a very good maid."

Jenna opened and closed her mouth uncertainly. She dipped her head in an awkward bow. "It is my duty, ma'am."

She could not have backed out of the room fast enough.

When she was gone, Bronwyn rose abruptly to her feet to throw open the doors to her wardrobe. She rifled carelessly through it, shoving the elegant, expensive gowns aside as though they were nothing more than cheap muslin. When she found her best green gown, she spun away from the wardrobe without bothering to re-order the crumpled dresses.

She dressed herself in the rich, emerald silk dress. It contoured perfectly to her plump bosom and full, curved hips, displaying her hour-glass figure for him as though he did not already know what waited, as though he had not already sampled her yielding flesh and the taste of her salty arousal.

But he had not. It had not been her body he had ravaged. She had merely received the echo of his attentions in her wildest, most erotic dreams.

Tonight it would be real.

She twisted her hair into a careful plait and wrapped it around the crown of her head. Her pale neck looked long and graceful. It looked inviting. Her lips curved into a humorless smile. She did not blush her cheeks with rouge or paint her lips. She secured dangling diamond earrings in her ears and a small, glittering pendant around her neck. The pointed tip of the tiny diamonds, set into a delicate triangle, brushed the tops of her breasts above her neckline.

She rose and spun away from the mirror. She sat quietly upon the window seat. Her mind shut down. She did not sleep, but she did not question or reconsider her decision. She waited patiently.

Night fell, and, with it, silence upon the house.

Bronwyn rose from her seat. She smoothed her gown and patted her hair. She was ready. She lifted her chin and stole silently out into the night.

* * *

Bronwyn ignored the shocked stares she received as she strode purposefully through the main streets of the East End. Despite the borough's reputation, no one stepped forward to bother or accost her. Perhaps the way her dark eyes flashed warned them to stay away. She was on an evil errand, and even the lowest lives of the East End wanted nothing to do with her.

She met a tall, thin man in a tattered suit in the entrance to a dark alley. He stared at her for a long moment, as though he was unsure what to do with her. She looked at him with a cold, flat gaze. There was murder, death and despair in her eyes. There was nothing left to lose.

He backed slowly away into the alley.

No one else came near. They let her pass swiftly by. They shrunk away from her as though she might suddenly turn on them and attack. She did not pause. She knew exactly where to find him, as though by instinct or scent. His man had given her his location with a slight, gleaming smirk as though he suspected her errand or was amused by the determination in her eyes. He had been expecting her. She had seen the triumph in his eyes. His master had played her like a fine instrument.

It didn't matter. Even if the monster had planned it all along, it didn't matter.

The Rusted Scabbard Tavern was noisy when she approached the dark, dirty alley. Men and women spilled out into the streets, talking, laughing and kissing each other. The men groped indecently at the women's breasts and lifted skirts. The women smiled and cooed at them with gleaming, hungry eyes. Somewhere in the deepest shadows, Bronwyn heard a woman moaning lustily while a man grunted in rhythm. The prostitutes striding slowly along the main thoroughfare outside were beautiful and well-dressed. Bronwyn wondered from what society the women came.

She did not speak to them. They looked up at her uncertainly as she approached. They seemed not to know if she was a new fallen angel come to work the streets with them. They did know she did not belong. They backed away from her to allow her to pass.

She did not go inside. She paused under a faint, flickering street torch and waited.

Lord Rafael was before her in moments. He smiled that slow burning smile that caused her to feel as though a flame had licked at her core. "I knew you would come." His voice was low and husky. It ran over her body like a moth's wing caress.

She hated him for what he did to Alys, but she wanted him so badly, her body quivered and shook as she held back from throwing herself at his feet and offering everything to him. She was not looking at a man. She was looking at a monster.

He reached for her. Arousal pulsed through her. The memory of his touch in her dream was nothing. He wrapped his arms around her waist and drew her up against his long, lean torso. She could already feel his arousal straining through his trousers and brushing across her belly. She yearned for it, to feel its weight in her hand, in her mouth, inside her. She had never known these feelings before.

She had not realized they had moved, but he was suddenly lying her down on a massive bed. A very gentle breeze rustled the heavy black drapes opened to the full, plump moon outside. She did not know where they were. She did not care.

Rafael held himself above her. He stared down into her eyes. His eyes were so large, they seemed to see all of her, her very desires. They swallowed her. He seemed to know exactly what she wanted. He brushed a hand down her cheek in such a tender gesture, her belly flipped. He smiled and leaned down to press a kiss to her temple, to her cheek, her mouth. It was the same gentle, shattering kiss that he had given her the night before, before he'd taken Alys for the last time and killed her.

She trembled and ached for him. This time, it would be real. She curled her fingers on his back, sliding her hands down to squeeze his firm, smooth bottom. She had never touched a man before. She had never been so brazen before. She didn't care. He chuckled low in his throat and ground against her. She felt his rigid cock through his trousers, through the silky folds of her dress.

She wanted it inside her.

He was in no hurry. Despite his intense arousal, sex did not seem to be at the forefront of his mind. He brushed his lips softly against hers. "I have been waiting so long for you," he whispered against her mouth. His tongue darted out to tease her lower lip, but when she opened her mouth to stroke it with her own, he pulled back slightly. "I am going to make you feel so alive. I'm going to show you everything in the world."

His words were as seductive as his body against hers. She dropped her head back and sighed. He made a small, choked noise in the back of his throat. When she opened her eyes to look back at him, his upper lip was skinned back like an angry dog's. His teeth glistened in the moonlight. Fear snaked through her belly, but it was far too late to rethink her decision. His fangs lengthened.

He cradled her head gently in his hands and dipped his head to her neck. She jolted in pain as his teeth pierced her flesh. She whimpered and clutched at him. He grunted savagely and ground his cock between her legs as he sucked powerfully at her neck. Her body rocked. She placed her hands on his shoulders to push him away from her, but he was as solid and unmovable as a stone.

He growled low in his throat. Heat and need coursed through her veins. She moaned and moved her hips restlessly against him. He did not unfasten his teeth from her neck, but he reached between them and tore her dress in two with no effort at all. He fumbled to shove her clothing away from her body, to bare her to his hands and his own flesh. His fingers brushed across the swollen throbbing nub between her legs. She cried out. It didn't feel the way it had in her dream. It was better. It was more powerful, more intense.

He freed himself from his trousers and shoved her legs apart. He entered her roughly. Pain lanced through her. He was larger than he had been in her dreams, or she had not known how it would feel the first time. She cried out and shoved at him, but he ignored her, pinning her wrists beside her head. He never lifted his mouth from her neck.

She felt her limbs going weak and rubbery, but the pain where he drove relentlessly inside her, mindlessly pounding towards his own completion suddenly abated. The tension building up inside her felt for a moment like pain, and then it exploded around her. She screamed out, but her words were incomprehensible. Above her, Rafael suddenly growled out in his own pleasure. He lifted his head and bared his teeth to the ceiling like a dog. Her blood glistened on his mouth. Her muscles pulsed and tightened around his long, hard cock. She saw stars.

She came silently, her head thrown back and her teeth gritted against the sensations rolling over her. In the same moment, she died.

Chapter One

A cloud of acrid grey smoke filled the air. It obscured the bookshelves behind the large, round marble-topped table in the center of the laboratory. The clear glass computer screens along the north east wall fogged up. Fallon Weir curled her lip and waved her hand in the air to clear it. She spun in her chair and glared at Gregor Blaize.

"There's no smoking in here," Skye Blayne growled as he strode into the room. Behind his round, rimless glasses, his large, pale blue eyes glared at the tall, slender man leaning back in a chair and blowing smoke into the air from a long, thin cigarette.

Gregor tossed his wavy dark hair. "Since when?" His voice was a melodic purr.

"Smoking kills, Gregor."

He lifted a perfectly arched eyebrow. "It won't kill me."

"We aren't all immortal."

Fallon scowled at him. "Put it out, Greg. I hate when you smoke in here. It leaves a greasy yellow film all over my screens."

Gregor sighed and snuffed the hot tip of the cigarette out in his cupped palm. His skin sizzled. He did not even wince. The wound healed instantly and he tossed the butt into the small trash can beside the case housing their collection of swords, knives, crossbows, guns and both arcane and cutting edge weaponry.

Fallon spun back to her computer screens. Her thin, pale red lips pursed slightly in irritation. Her long, slender fingers flew over the flat glass console in front of her. On the large, glass screen above her head, images and words flew across the glass so rapidly, it was a wonder she could read them at all.

Gregor leaned back in his chair and clutched his head dramatically. "I'm so bored! When is Remy coming back?"

Fallon scowled without turning to face him. "How should I know?"

"How long can it take to bag a wolf?"

"As long as it takes," Skye snapped irritably. He sat down beside Fallon at his own screen. His fingers moved more slowly, and he studied the strange, ancient writing on his monitor with an expression of deep concentration.

Fallon sighed and rubbed her large, watery blue eyes. She looked as though she hadn't slept in a few days. There were dark circles under her eyes. Her stunning face looked haggard, and her long, moonlight pale blonde hair was stringy as though she hadn't tended to it in a while. She needed a few square meals and a long night's sleep.

Skye cut a sideways glance at her. His tone was quiet when he spoke, but he might as well have shouted. Gregor's sensitive ears would pick up every word. "You look tired, Fallon. Are you feeling all right?"

Her brow contracted as though the question bothered her. "I'm fine."

Gregor eyed her shrewdly. Her skin was so pale, it was almost translucent. Her hands shook almost undetectably on the keys of her flat glass keyboard. He knew she'd been taking the juice again. The evidence of her addiction was undeniable. She was still beautiful now, but it would not be long before she lost the glow of her youth and health. He sighed.

Noah Murdock stomped into the room. His long, curved katana blade dribbled drops of thick, coagulated blood across the hardwood floor. A large bruise was already purpling his left eye. There were deep, jagged cuts in the tanned skin of his well-muscled arms. He wiped the blade carelessly with a blood-soaked cloth from his back pocket and lifted it onto the shelf.

"Noah!" Skye snapped, aghast. "Clean the blade before you return it to its place. What will this laboratory become when it's covered in vamp blood?"

"Stinky," Fallon remarked.

Gregor stiffened indignantly. "Human blood is much stinkier than vampire blood, I will have you know."

Fallon rolled her eyes, but she did not reply.

"Where's Remy?" Noah asked.

Skye glared at him. "He isn't back yet. In case all of you have forgotten, he is not the one who runs this place. He wouldn't even be here if he didn't still have five years on his sentence."

Fallon lifted her chin. "Remy likes us. He likes it here."

Skye shrugged. "Maybe." He turned back to Noah and Gregor. "If you want something to do, I have plenty of cleaning and reorganizing of the supply closet to do since we had that mix-up with the vervain and sodium during Noah's purification ritual."

They all turned away. "Oh, I think I see some readings that need analyzing..." Fallon said.

"I have some research to do," Gregor added, dropping his feet to the ground and rolling toward his computer.

"Ah, I heard about a lead on that Japanese vamp we've been wanting to question..." Noah put in.

Skye rolled his eyes. "Children."

"We're the U.S. government," Fallon complained. "Can't we outsource?"

"We're the U.S. government. We don't have the budget for a maid." Skye flicked his fingers at them dismissively. "Move along. I actually have work to do. I want to get some research on that order of dark wizards in Chinatown."

"Aren't there people for that there?"

"The Agency does not officially recognize the vigilante groups in Chinatown. The official wants a briefing on what we are doing about them."

A door slammed in the lobby downstairs. A man's voice murmured calmly over the sounds of angry snarling. The team perked up. Skye sighed. He rose to join the others as they descended the stairs to the large reception area. It was a large, two-story room with a pointed cathedral ceiling and two staircases on either side that met upstairs at a loft that once housed a large collection of books.

The San Francisco duty station of the Secret Service Paranormal Sector had been a library until it had been destroyed several years ago in a battle between rival warlock gangs. It still looked a bit like a library, but most of the bookshelves had been burnt in a fire or removed to make room for the intricate laboratory and training facilities. The floors were polished blue marble with flecks of black and white. It still bore the scratches and signs of the battle, but the Agency had taken care to restore the building.

Skye wasn't sure why. The people who worked in it hardly regarded the painstaking efforts or even bothered to take care not to cause further damage.

A tall, well-built man with wavy, dark blonde, chin-length hair brushed back from a strong, chiseled face guided his struggling captive into the lobby in handcuffs. Remy St. John's jeans were scuffed and ripped in the knees, and there were scratches on his handsome face. He was scowling.

His prisoner looked worse. Bloody lacerations streaked his face, arms and legs, and his clothes were in torn, bloody tatters. He looked only half human. His face and limbs were covered in patches of thick, dark grey hair. His nose was wide like a snout, and his teeth looked razor sharp as he peeled back his lips to snarl at the team when they arrived. His fingernails were dirty, ragged claws. He looked as though Remy had snapped the magic-inhibiting cuffs on him either as he'd changed from human to wolf or back again.

Remy could probably have cuffed him before the change or waited until it had ended, but fighting werewolves was a lot more fun than tangling with humans.

When the half-man, half-wolf spoke, it was in a growl. "I didn't do anything. You have no right to detain me."

Remy flipped a stray lock of hair out of his large, electric blue eyes. An aura of dark energy swirled around him in an almost tangible fog. "Yeah, yeah. You've got all the time in the world to tell us your story. You aren't going anywhere anytime soon."

The team strode forward to meet them. "Can I help?" Noah asked. He was shorter than Remy by a couple inches, but he was more thickly muscled. His dark hair was closely cropped, and there were scars on his even, deeply tanned features. The wolf-man barely flinched as he approached. He almost leaned toward him, as though eager to escape his captor, even if it meant asylum with the ex-soldier.

Remy shrugged and propelled his prisoner toward Noah. "Sure. Kennel him."

Noah smirked a little and tugged the wolf-man out of the lobby toward the holding cells in the basement. The prisoner complained bitterly as they went. Noah ignored him. If he was lucky, the ex-soldier would let him change back into a human shape before he was shoved into one of the magic-dampening cells to await his fate.

Noah probably wouldn't.

Fallon and Gregor strode forward to meet Remy as he turned to them. They looked as though they had hardly been able to wait for him to return. He lifted an eyebrow and crossed his arms across his broad, flatly-muscled chest. His black v-neck tee-shirt was torn down the side, revealing the firm skin beneath. Fallon's eyes raked across his body with a burning, desperate hunger. Remy didn't seem to notice.

Somewhere behind them, the paranormal radar blipped. No one noticed.

"Hey, Rem," Gregor said. His beautiful, sculpted face split into a grin. His teeth glistened a brilliant, unnatural white in the florescent lights above. His dark, almond shaped eyes glittered as though the scent of blood on his teammate and the prisoner had aroused him. His voice was a deep, husky purr. "How was the hunt?"

Remy didn't seem bothered by Gregor's bloodlust. He shrugged. "Lame. He tried to leap off the Golden Gate Bridge to get away. He thought I wouldn't follow him."

"That explains the smell," Gregor remarked.

"Wet dog," Fallon complained with a grimace. "Ick."

Remy rolled his eyes, but his full, sculpted mouth turned up in a half-smile. He lifted the corner of his tattered tee-shirt. Fallon's and Gregor's eyes followed his movement raptly. "I'm going to change. Anything new going on here?"

"Nah," Gregor replied sullenly. "Nothing. It's been extremely dull around here. There's nothing to do."

Skye cleared his throat to remind them he was still in the room. "There is still the small issue of the explosion in the ritual lab."

"Can't we hire someone to take care of that?" Remy asked.

"Skye's too cheap," Fallon told him.

Skye drew himself up to his full height. He was well over six feet, but he was so slender, he seemed much shorter. "It isn't in the budget."

Remy rolled his eyes. "Yeah. We'll get right on it, then."

Something in his tone suggested the ritual lab was going to remain dirty for the next several years.

* * *

Noah leaned back in his chair with his feet propped up on the glass console. His head lulled against his thick chest as he dozed. He grunted softly in his sleep and swiped at his face as though he felt a fly land on it. He might have been dreaming.

The screen in front of him switched on. On a radar map of the city, a small red blip appeared in the center. Then it was gone.

Noah jolted awake, dropping his feet heavily to the ground. He shook his head as if to clear it. The screen in front of him was quiet and blank. He sighed in disappointment. There was nothing to do.

He called up the local daily newspapers and scanned the headlines. He lifted his eyebrows in interest, then sighed. Trouble in Pacific Heights did not turn out to be a demon infestation or a vamp nest. It was nothing more than an outbreak of lice amongst the children. It was an infestation, at least.

He scrolled through the crime section compulsorily. There didn't seem to be anything of interest to the Agency, although he did normally enjoy reading about what the normal police did all day in their city. There seemed to be a lot of public intoxication and lewd behavior lately. He paused and went back to the article he'd just skimmed. He frowned at the screen.

The reporter was Leda Bowles, San Francisco's unofficial correspondent to the strange. Her feature was tiny, hidden among the lists of arrests and reported crimes. *Another body was found yesterday in a dark alley in the Tenderloin. The victim is one of five killed in the same way in as many weeks. Sources at the coroner's office have concluded the cause of death is attack by a wild animal due to the nature of the injuries. Teeth and claw marks were discovered on all five victims. Police and animal control have yet to determine what sort of animal is responsible for the attacks...*

Noah perked up. Animal attacks were right up his alley. There was almost always something more interesting going on. He was dying for interesting. It had been a slow couple of weeks. Hunting down and killing murderous vamps and werewolves was fun, but there was more interesting game. If he was lucky, it would turn out to be a rare demon crossing through the dimensions and taking a few hapless victims along the way. If he was unlucky, it would be a very eager young werewolf.

Either way, it was better than being cooped up in the office all day long.

He jumped up and shouted out into the hallway. "Remy!"

Skye's head snapped up from his screen. "Why are you shouting? We have an intercom."

Noah ignored him. "This is important."

"What is it?"

"Some attacks in the Tenderloin. The police haven't identified the attacker. They think it might be some kind of wild animal."

Skye stared at him for several seconds. His thin mouth pursed. "Why are you calling Remy? I'm right here."

Noah looked as though he didn't understand the question. He looked up eagerly as Remy strode into the room. His dark blonde hair was still wet from a shower and combed back from his blue eyes. He lifted an eyebrow.

"What's up, Noah?"

Noah pointed toward his computer screen. "Have you see the Daily?"

"No. There something we should know about?"

"There have been some unusual attacks."

Remy skimmed the article swiftly. Skye rose to read over his shoulder. Remy nodded slowly. "Looks like we'd better go talk to Leda and find out if there's something we should know about all this."

Skye frowned. "I wonder that we haven't already been informed about this. The PD usually notifies us when there has been this many attacks in this short of a time span."

Remy smirked. "What do you say, boss? Should we go check it out?"

Skye lifted his chin at Remy's slightly patronizing tone. "Yes. Go speak to Miss Bowles. I will contact the other duty stations and see if anyone else has heard of something like this."

"There's not much to go on."

"No, but if the local authorities haven't identified the animal yet, it could be something we haven't seen before. They have records of our sort of creatures. If they had recognized it, they would have called us."

Noah's eyes gleamed at the idea. He looked eagerly at Remy. Remy nodded. "Let's go. It's better than hanging around here with nothing to do, anyway. If it sounds promising, we can stop by the coroner's office."

They turned toward the door in the same moment Fallon barreled into the room. She looked awful. Her eyes were rimmed in dark circles, and her mascara had smeared down her cheeks as though she had been crying. Her cheeks looked hollow. Her eyes, though, gleamed with a mad, burning light.

"I've had a vision," she announced.

Noah stepped forward to catch her shoulders. Gregor appeared in the doorway behind her with an interested expression. He must have heard Fallon's pronouncement from wherever he'd been lurking. "What is it, Fallon?" Noah asked anxiously.

"A woman." Her tone was slightly dreamy.

"Is she hurt?"

"No. She's--she's hurting people. She's a vampire."

Remy frowned. "You're sure?"

"Yes. I saw her fangs."

"Who is she?" Gregor asked in interest.

Fallon shook her head. "I don't know who she is. I know what she looks like. I can describe her."

Skye nodded decisively. "Fallon, you sit down with Gregor. You can plug the description in the database, see if we can figure out who she is."

"You think she's important?" Noah asked.

"I don't know, but she's close," Fallon replied. "I think she was in Soma. One of the underground vamp bars."

"Killing?" Gregor asked. His voice was low and husky. He missed killing.

Fallon sighed deeply. Her shoulders slumped. "I'm not sure. I saw her feeding."

Gregor sighed in disappointment. "She could have found a willing donor at one of the bars. She might be harmless."

They looked at him doubtfully.

"What?"

"No vamp is harmless," Noah said darkly.

Gregor lifted his shoulders with a smirk.

Remy turned and strode toward the door. "We'll talk to Leda. Fallon, you and Gregor figure out who the vamp is."

"Interesting timing," Noah remarked. "She might have something to do with the killings."

"What killings?" Gregor demanded. "There's been killings? We have a case now?"

"Maybe," Skye replied. "We haven't determined whether it falls in our sector or not." He glanced pointedly at Remy and Noah over his rimless glasses. "We'll know more when we've talked to Leda."

"Right. We're on it."

Remy and Noah started out the door. Remy suddenly spun around and strode abruptly toward Fallon. He caught her shoulders. She looked up at him with a wild, glazed expression. "Are you on the juice?" he asked in a low growl.

She tossed her long, blonde hair. "I don't know what you're talking about."

"Yes, you do."

"Leave me alone, Remy. You have no right to talk to me about that."

He sighed. She tugged out of his grasp and stormed out of the room. She was right; he didn't have any right to talk about that at all. He was no better than she was. Skye and Gregor ignored them, but Noah looked after Fallon as though he was considering going after her.

"Is she okay?" Noah asked. His brow furrowed. "She's taking the stuff again?"

Remy nodded. "Yeah. I think so."

Noah cursed.

"Her abilities are killing her, Noah. The more she uses them, the more they take away what life she has left.

Noah scowled. "Taking the junk isn't going to help."

"No. It isn't. But it takes away the pain."

Noah's expression was sharp. "How come you don't have any pain?"

"It's different." Remy turned away from him to stride back toward the door. "I'll pay the price for what I did."

They didn't speak about it again as Remy drove across the city to the San Francisco Daily office. They were silent as they walked inside and flashed their badges at the receptionist. They didn't need to explain themselves. "Leda's in her office," the young woman told them. She smiled at them, and then she turned back to her computer without a second glance. Her fingers moved so rapidly over the keys, Remy was concerned the keyboard might ignite.

The young, dark-haired girl must have alerted Leda on their way through the rows of desks. The tall, thick middle-aged woman met them at the door bearing her name. Her thick, bright red lips curled into a smile. "I wondered when you were going to show up. I expected you much sooner than after the fifth victim."

Leda was a sassy old broad with a twisted sense of humor. She needed it. She had been unofficially assigned the Freak Beat years ago when it became clear she was the only reporter on the Daily, perhaps even in San Francisco, who could deal with the nuances and the horrors of the paranormal community day in and day out without tipping over the edge. She was also the only reporter in town that had enough sense not to go around shouting about vamps and wolves and the rest of the weirdness they dealt with everyday.

Not everyone knew about the paranormal community. Leda had a knack for keeping those that did know what was going on in their world in the loop while ensuring the rest of the population didn't learn enough to turn into a full-scale mob with torches, silver bullets and wooden stakes. She was good, and she was always eager to help the Secret Service.

She had a short, fire-engine red bob that matched her full, painted lips. Most days, she wore black, and it suited her. Today she was wearing a no-nonsense black suit. She looked a bit like a comic book character. She grinned at them and crooked her finger to beckon them into her office. It was a large room with a good view of the city below. Leda was well-known, well-respected and well-paid.

Her office was decorated in black wood, wire and chrome. She liked spindly chairs and shining surfaces. Abstract art in bright primary colors punctuated the stark neutral tones of the furniture. Leda leaned back in her tall, black leather chair and peered at them over the top of her bright red laptop. Her fingernails were short and as blood red as her lips.

Remy lifted an eyebrow. "You're sure all five victims were killed by the same creature?"

Leda gave him an arch look. "Don't look at me because you people haven't been paying attention to the streets. Yes, I'm sure. I was on the scene all five times."

He inclined his head and lifted a hand as if to beckon her to continue. She smirked slightly and folded her hands in front of her. He sighed. "What can you tell us about the killings?"

She grinned. "The victims were all found in dirty alleys in the Tenderloin. It didn't seem as though they were dumped there after they were killed. They died where they were found."

Remy and Noah glanced at each other. "Is there anything special about the alleys? Do they have a common element?" Remy asked.

"They've all been heavily populated night spots. Areas with lots of bars and restaurants. Plenty of people. Typical hunting grounds." She opened a drawer in her desk and extracted a thin file. It had Remy's name on the tab. She'd printed out her notes for him. She had been waiting for them. "So this is one of your things, then?"

"Maybe," Noah replied, peering over Remy's shoulder to read Leda's crisp cursive hand.

"Who is the officer on the case?" Remy asked.

"There is no case. Not yet. The PD still wants to believe it's an animal attack. You know how they are when it comes to the Freak Beat."

Noah rolled his eyes. "What sort of animal do they think did this?"

"Can't say, really. No one has come up with anything conclusive yet. It looks like a wolf, but there's no blood on the scene. It's been drained."

Noah frowned. "Vamps don't maul and wolves don't drain."

Leda smiled and inclined her head as though he'd solved a very elaborate puzzle.

"God, it could be both," Noah muttered. "That would be a hell of a thing."

"It could be something totally new." Leda looked as though she wasn't sure whether to be excited or appalled by this idea. "There's a crime scene guy working the autopsies. A new guy in the lab. He's trying to determine the type of animal responsible for the attacks so animal control can go hunt them down."

"You got a name?"

"Pete Strader."

"Yeah. I know him. We worked a couple wolf attacks together a couple months ago. He's all right. "Remy rose abruptly."Thanks, Leda."

She pursed her plump red lips. "Just remember who helped you."

"You bet." He nodded to her and jerked his head at Noah.

"You want to talk to the crime scene guy?" the soldier asked as they left the Daily offices.

"Yeah."

Noah didn't look as if this was the answer he'd been hoping for. "I want to call the office and see if they have an ID on the vamp in Fallon's vision. It could be connected. She could be responsible."

Remy gave him a shrewd sideways glance. "You said it yourself. Vamps don't maul."

"Some vamps rip their victims to pieces. It wouldn't be the first time one of them was doing something violent and deranged."

Remy smirked. "All right." He dialed the office number from the SUV's speaker phone. Gregor's voice filled the car.

"Hey, Rem."

"Any lead on that vamp in Fallon's vision?" Noah asked without offering a greeting.

Gregor sighed long-sufferingly, as though Noah had deeply insulted him. "Yeah. Looks like it's Bronwyn Liddle. An old vamp."

"What do we know about her?" Remy asked as he steered the SUV toward the Medical Examiner's office.

"A lot, actually. She was vamped in the early 1800's by a vampire named Rafael Zubiri."

"Never heard of him."

"No. You wouldn't have. He died about a hundred years ago. Bronwyn killed him."

"She killed her sire? That doesn't happen very often."

"Yeah, well, we know what she did; we don't know why she did it."

"Okay. You think she might have something to do with the killings?"

"Nothing in her file suggests either way. She's not known for tearing apart her victims." Gregor paused, and when he spoke again, it sounded as though he was smiling. "You might want to take a look at the profile, Rem."

He frowned. "Why?"

"She's an old friend of the *Castus Vox*."

"And old friend?" Remy's voice sounded skeptical.

"Well, she met them once. It might have been friendly before everyone died."

Remy lifted his eyebrows. "She killed them?"

"Not sure. It doesn't say, but she was there when about a dozen *Castus Vox* were killed."

He considered this. "What else do you have?"

"She's got a few known contacts around the city we can talk to. The usual vamps and mages. They might know what she's doing here."

"Anyone we know?"

"Yeah. She's been seen around the Bleeding Orchid in Soma a few times. She's had a few meetings with Merek."

"What for?"

"I have no idea. You'd have to ask him. He works mostly for us."

"He's an information broker," Noah put in darkly. "He's known for selling out his own kind."

"If he was, he wouldn't still be alive," Gregor said sharply.

They didn't say anything for several moments, until Remy said musingly, "She killed her sire. You think she's a vampire hunter?"

"Could be. It's not unheard of. You'd have to have real self loathing issues to hunt your own people."

Noah scoffed. "You hunt your own kind."

"I hunt criminals. I don't discriminate based on their sub-species."

"That's fair."

"Anything else I should know?" Remy asked.

"There isn't much personal information. No philosophy or affiliations, but she's been connected to the Irish witch Cicely."

Remy raised his eyebrows. "Cicely? She's still around?"

"Sure she is. She's always been around. Either she's found a potion for immortality or she's not human."

"That not our problem. She's not in our jurisdiction."

"The Irish people don't seem to mind her. She's considered an ally."

Remy frowned. "We don't know anything about Bronwyn."

"Not really. We can ask around and find out what she's been to see Merek about."

"It might not be anything we need to look into. She might just be looking up an old friend. It happens."

Noah scowled. "Right, so why is Fallon having visions about her?"

Gregor's voice was low. "She's juicing. I think she's having visions of tomorrow's breakfast, amongst other things."

"Does Skye know?" Remy asked.

"Of course he does. He always knows."

Remy nodded. "We need to do something about her before it gets too bad."

"It's not our job right now." Gregor sounded irritated. "Have you heard anything useful about the killings?"

"Nothing we can do anything with. The victims have been mauled like a wolf but their blood has been drained like a vamp. It could still be either one," Noah explained. "We're going to talk to the crime scene investigator. Maybe they got some trace that would help us focus our attention on one or the other."

"It could just be an animal."

"How often is it just an animal?"

"That's a fair point. Well, good luck. I'll let Skye know where you've gone." He was silent a moment. "I'm going to sleep. When night falls, I'll go talk to Merek and see what he knows about Bronwyn Liddle."

"If I'm done with the investigation, I'll go with you," Remy put in.

"Why? It doesn't sound related to your case."

"Maybe it is; maybe it isn't. Merek usually has information we don't even know we need."

"Okay. If you want to come, I'm not going to stop you. Have fun with the crime scene guy." He paused. "Those guys give me the creeps."

Remy chuckled and pressed a button on the steering wheel to end the call. His expression was far away as he drove them through the winding, hilly streets toward the center of town. "So Fallon's vamp is Bronwyn Liddle."

Noah shrugged. This information didn't seem to interest him in the least. His even, rugged featured contracted into a scowl. "We need to do something about Fallon."

Remy glanced at him. "Okay. We will. I promise."

This snapped Noah out of his fugue. He glanced at his partner with a sharp expression. "So, Greg and Fallon don't think Bronwyn has anything to do with the killings."

Remy shrugged. "No way to know until we've figured out what she's doing here. It sounds like she might be a hunter. I want to know more about her before we jump to any conclusions about what she's doing here and if she's connected

46

to all this."

"Right." Noah scowled. "Let's get on with it then. I want to get this case over with. It leaves a bad taste in my mouth in more ways than one."

* * *

The receptionist at the Medical Examiner's office didn't even glance at their badges as they strode into the lobby. She recognized them immediately. She lifted an eyebrow and smiled at them. "I suppose you're here to ask about the attacks?"

Noah and Remy exchanged a glance. Remy crossed his arms over his chest and gave Thea Rose a smoldering look. She flushed. "Any particular reason we should? Have you heard anything about them?"

Thea fluttered her hand over her chest. She was a slender woman in her early twenties with long, dark hair. She was pretty, and her smile was dazzling. Thea chewed bubblegum and did her college class work at her desk. She wasn't studying to work in the ME's office. She wanted to be a psychologist. She was in the right place to get some experience. "Nah. I wish I had. Since they got the bulletproof glass, I don't hear as much as I used to, and Strader doesn't tell me anything."

Noah smirked. "Bulletproof glass?"

She tilted her head over her shoulder at the thick pane of sparkling clear glass behind her desk. Beyond, it the Medical Examiner's office was bustling with people in lab coats moving in and out of labs and offices and pushing around gurneys. Some of the gurneys were laden with human-shaped body bags. They looked full. "We've had a lot of threats after the incidents in Chinatown."

Remy's full, sculpted mouth turned up slightly at the corners. "How come you aren't behind the glass?"

She rolled her eyes. "I wondered the same thing myself. Apparently, it's an acceptable risk. I'm worth the least if someone comes in here shooting." She shook her head, but she turned her high-voltage smile back on them. She didn't really expect anyone to come in shooting, or she probably would have walked right out the door. "Anyway, I heard a little about the attacks. There aren't many animals in San Francisco that could or would do that to a person. And when it's something like this, it's usually one of your things."

"Yeah. It's starting to sound like it," Noah agreed. He sounded a little too excited.

"Is Strader around?" Remy asked.

Thea nodded. "Yeah. He's in the lab. He checked in a few hours ago. I'll buzz him and let him know you're coming in."

"Thanks, Thea."

The heavy, high-security door buzzed noisily. Thea jerked her head at it and picked up the phone to call Strader as Remy and Noah strode inside the office. It was as though a sound barrier had lifted. Police detectives talked to medical examiners and lab techs; bereaved family members mourned and just as often cursed their lost loved ones. Remy and Noah waved around at the officers and lab techs they knew, but they didn't pause to talk to anyone. They didn't have many friends in local law enforcement.

In fact, no one looked that pleased to see them. They looked up at them warily as they passed.

A tall man with closely cropped dark hair and deep wrinkles in a tanned face strode out to meet them. Even though his hands were swathed in gloves and he wore goggles on his forehead, he didn't look like one of the lab geeks. He looked tough and rugged, as though he spent a lot of time outside. His shoulders were broad and his arms were thickly muscled. He didn't look as though he was happy to see them, but he nodded politely at them. He must have noticed his co-workers' frowns. He jerked his head to guide them into his lab.

"I expected you a lot sooner." Strader was a no-nonsense matter-of-fact kind of man. He rarely spoke unless it involved a case, but he always knew something no one else had figured out yet.

Remy liked him. "Yeah? I heard you're working the series of animal attacks."

"That's right." He gestured around him to encompass the Petri dishes lying around him in a sort of spiral arrangement. If he had a method of organizing them, Remy couldn't see it.

Remy jerked his chin toward the microscope in the midst of the Petri dish chaos. "What can you tell us?"

Strader's expression remained impassive. "It's definitely your area. I was about to call."

Remy lifted his eyebrows. "What sort of creature is it?"

Strader shook his head. "I don't know."

"What do you mean you don't know? What's all this, then?"

The lab tech shrugged. "I almost hate to give up this case, even though they're the most horrifying animal attacks I've ever seen."

"Come on."

Strader shrugged. "What people do to people is awful. Worse than what animals do to people. This, though, isn't like what animals or people do to people. The victims have been torn to shreds. But this was done after all the blood had been drained from them."

"So the killer--"

Strader cut Noah off. "I'm not sure it can be called that. It definitely isn't human."

Noah rolled his eyes. "So the attacker drained them, then mauled them."

"Right."

"Any fang marks?"

"It's hard to say. The marks on the victims indicate sharp teeth as well as claws."

"It could still be a wolf," Noah muttered. He sounded disappointed.

"It could be," Strader agreed positively. "It was actually."

"It was? Why didn't you say so?" Remy demanded.

"There's more to it than that." Strader gestured toward the microscope. "I did discover hair on the bodies."

"Wolf hair." Remy sighed. He'd had enough of werewolves.

"Yes. Two different kinds."

"What?"

"One is a werewolf breed. The other is unknown. It's probably a breed we haven't identified in the database yet."

Noah frowned. "So there's more than one attacker."

"No. The same hairs were found on all the victims, but there is no indication this is a pack attack."

"Not to mention, the breeds usually don't mix."

"Right. The injuries are consistent with only one attacker."

"You're saying the creature is two types of werewolf at the same time."

"There's more." Strader's dark eyes gleamed. "Look at this." He swapped the slide in the microscope and gestured toward it.

Remy peered into the eyepiece. When he lifted his head, he frowned and glanced at Noah, who dipped his head to see what had caused his partner's expression. "It's scales."

"Yes. Like some kind of reptile," Strader replied, bobbing his head.

"What the hell, man?" Noah asked.

"It's not any kind of reptile I've seen. The pattern of the scale is all wrong."

Remy and Noah exchanged another glance. "Traces of the scales were found on all five victims?" Remy asked.

Strader looked as though he'd been waiting for this question. His eyes gleamed. "Actually, the bits of scales are spliced with the hairs."

Remy blinked. Noah scowled. "Okay, what?"

"I discovered some of these scales and some trace that appears to be part scale, part hair."

"How the hell is that possible?"

"I wouldn't know."

"You're saying there is some creature out there that is two parts wolf and one part reptile?"

"Right."

"That's new."

"It could be some sort of genetic splicing. I've seen it before."

"Yeah, in cartoons," Remy growled.

Noah grinned. "I love that cartoon, man. Man, people are crazy." He scowled suddenly at Strader as though he was putting them on. "Are you saying there's some scientist out there splicing weres with de-reptiles?"

Remy glanced at him sharply. It was generally best not to say the D-word, even around the police. They tended to get a glazed or hunted expression like the SS was playing some great joke on them. Or like they hoped they were. He looked back at Strader. "Thanks for the tip, man."

Strader lifted a wry eyebrow. "I suppose you'll be taking over from here?"

"You know the drill." Strader sighed and began stacking the Petri dishes in a red plastic container. Remy took it from him. "The file, too."

"You guys suck." He handed the thick case file to Noah. "You'll have to sign for it."

Remy didn't like signing his name to anything. He tipped his head at Noah, who rolled his eyes and scribbled on the clipboard Strader placed in front of him. "Thanks, Strader. You've been a real help."

Remy tilted his head toward the door, and Noah followed him, leaving Strader looking as though they had taken away his Lego Transformers play set. "Let's head to the morgue and talk to the medical examiner on the case. We might be able to learn more about the nature of the creature."

Noah shrugged. The morgue didn't seem to bother him. A deep, ominous chill enveloped them as they stepped out of the elevator into the basement of the ME's office building. Remy felt a shiver creep down his spine, but he ignored it. Noah seemed unaffected by the cold. He had braved far harsher conditions while in the service, and he wasn't easily perturbed. Remy's field experiences had typically included room service.

Dr. Emma Rue was already waiting for them when they arrived at the heavy metal door stamped with the word MORGUE in stark, impersonal letters. She pushed open the door to allow them inside and tilted her head. "Hello, gentleman."

Dr. Rue was a humorless woman with short, wavy dark hair and a stern face that might have been beautiful if it had been softer in expression. Her dark eyes were cold and clinical, and her features were strong. They were set permanently into a very slight frown. Her forehead was wrinkled where her brow contracted. She did not have smile lines around her mouth. Her jaw was rigid. Perhaps she had seen too much death.

"Dr. Rue." Remy inclined his head politely to her. She didn't like him. She didn't seem to like anyone, and she wasn't always helpful. He hoped she was in a giving mood. "We understand you're working the unusual animal attacks."

She spun on her heel and strode toward the covered body on her slab. "Yes, and I expected to see you here much sooner. There have already been five attacks. I suppose the Secret Service has better things to do."

Noah and Remy exchanged a frown. "Did everyone know before us?" Noah crossed his arms sullenly over his chest.

"As usual. What do you people do all day, anyway?"

Remy's lips tilted up into a very small smirk. "You wouldn't want to know."

Dr. Rue's mouth twitched so slightly, Remy thought it must have been his imagination. "I understand that."

"So, have you discovered anything we should know?"

She lifted her broad shoulders in a shrug. "It looks as though the victims are being bitten and drained of their blood. However, I found some traces of toxins in the bodies I couldn't identify."

"Toxins?"

"It bears a similarity to snake venom, but it isn't."

Noah frowned. "That's interesting." He glanced at Remy, but his partner seemed as stumped as he was.

"After they're poisoned and drained, the attacker tears them to shreds." Her dark eyes glittered. "Would you like to see?"

Remy leaned back. "I'm not sure about that."

Noah rolled his eyes. "Don't be a wuss."

Remy scowled at him, but he peered over the body as Dr. Rue drew the stark white sheet back from its face. It didn't have much of a face left. The skull was still intact, but the flesh hung in bloody, shredded ribbons from the bone. There was no sign of the victim's eyes. Its sockets looked black and vacant, but Remy thought he could still see the terror there, like a ghost pain in a severed limb.

Noah exhaled heavily and turned away from the body. Remy smirked. "Wuss."

Dr. Rue lifted an eyebrow. "Are you two finished?"

"I think we've seen enough."

"I'm already sending the tox and trace results to your database."

"Nice."

She flicked her fingers dismissively and turned back to her body. "See you."

They didn't bother to bid her goodbye. She wouldn't have acknowledged them, anyway. They spun and strode out of the morgue. They were relieved when the lift door closed and they ascended away from Dr. Rue and her charges.

"She's creepier than the bodies," Noah remarked.

"Not that body."

"Wuss." Noah glanced at him. "What do you think?"

"I don't know. Have you ever heard of anyone splicing monsters before?"

"Nah. I don't think they even could."

"I didn't think a werewolf could be vamped, either."

"No, they can't. They can be drained and killed, but they don't come back as a vamp. The blood is toxic to them. It just double kills them."

"Can you kill a werewolf with vamp blood?" Remy looked interested.

"I don't know. I suppose. In a large enough dose."

"And vamps cannot become werewolves."

"Nah. You think we're dealing with a demon?"

"Could be some breed we've never seen, but it seems to be all three. I want to see if there's any record of the toxin in the database. Our people might know something about it that can help us figure out what type of monster is responsible."

"Skye can run it through the system. There could even be some record of a mad scientist splicing monsters together into one big hybrid monster who can kill you six different ways."

Remy scowled. "If I find a deserted island with a bunch of misfit monsters spliced with chickens and poodles, I am going to lodge a complaint with the union."

"This job, man. It gets stupider every day."

#

Noah didn't wait for the front door to close before he demanded, "Where's Fallon?"

Remy shrugged and trailed behind him as he took the steps upstairs two at a time toward the second floor laboratory. Fallon was leaning back in her chair, reading documents on the large, glass screen in front of her. She glanced at them in surprise as Noah burst in. There were dark circles under her eyes, and she looked exhausted.

Her pale eyes were no longer glazed and glowing. They looked alert. She seemed almost better, even relaxed. Remy frowned. That wasn't good. It wouldn't be long before she crashed. It might happen at any moment.

Skye darted into the room. He lifted his eyebrows behind his rimless glasses. "Did you learn anything interesting?"

"Yeah. Very interesting, actually." Remy jerked his head. Noah handed Skye the red container. Remy spread the file out on the table. Skye glanced at it. A crease appeared in his brow. "The attacks are being committed by some sort of vamp/were/demon hybrid."

Skye blinked up at him. "I'm sorry?"

"CSI found two types of werewolf hair and unidentified scales. The victims were drained of their blood before they were mauled." He grimaced. "Shredded."

"Scales?" Fallon spun in her chair. She leaned her elbows on her knees.

"Yeah, and the tox screen showed some kind of venom," Noah added.

"So what is it, then?"

"A new kind of monster that's different kinds of monsters."

Skye stared at Noah without any expression on his face. "So what does this mean?"

"We're hunting a hybrid monster."

"Oh. Lovely. So what is your next step?"

Remy sighed. "I'm not sure whether to track it like a vamp, a were or a demon.

I don't know which creature is the dominant. Is there anything in the Agency archives about a mad scientist splicing monsters together?"

"Maybe. I'm still waiting to receive emails back from the other duty stations about any sort of similar attacks. Fallon and I can comb the databases for any mention of these sorts of monsters." He frowned thoughtfully. "This a bigger issue than I originally thought. I'm surprised we haven't heard about this already. I'm sure one of our people would have noticed traces of hybrid monsters if anyone's seen this before."

"It could be new," Remy said. He sighed and spun out one of the chairs to sit. He tilted it back to rest his feet on the table and crossed his arms over his chest. "This could be the first."

"How come we didn't cotton onto this sooner?" Fallon demanded. "I haven't heard a peep about hybrids."

"We were busy with the werewolf murder investigations."

"The local law could have tipped us off."

Noah scoffed. "I think they like to see us screw up as much as possible. They don't give anything up unless they have to."

"We know about it now," Skye said firmly. "Remy, Gregor left some information for you on your panel. He wants to talk to Merek when night falls."

"Right." Remy checked his watch. "I've got about two hours until twilight. Three until full dark." He lifted his hands to rub his eyes wearily. "I'm getting a sandwich."

* * *

There were no photographs of Bronwyn Liddle. The crude artist's rendering had been taken from an eyewitness account over a century ago. Remy was amazed it had lasted into the twentieth century to be scanned and uploaded into the Secret Service database. He supposed they'd kept very good records, even in the earliest days of the Agency's inception.

The sketch was kind, almost tender. Her long, auburn hair curled gently over her shoulders. Her large, dark, almond shaped-eyes looked soulful. She was beautiful. They were always beautiful. There was a certain quirk in her mouth, as though she knew someone was looking and liked what they saw. He wondered how accurate the sketch was. Did she actually wear that confident, sly expression?

Her profile was short. She'd been vamped in her late twenties in the early

1800's, and she'd spent the next hundred years or so traveling with her sire, Rafael. Most of the information had come from one of a network of Agency informants who had met her in a bar in Newark in the early 90's. The informants were paid well to gather intel on vamps, weres and other creatures of the night. They typically just hung out in the types of bars that drew paranormals and asked questions until they learned something useful.

It was not a bad way to get information. A lot of them knew some great tricks to get people to talk. A lot of them were paranormals themselves. Unfortunately, though it was often reliable enough, it was mostly hearsay and rumors, and there weren't many creatures who don't take an opportunity to boast when it's presented to them. Bronwyn's informant had been Gwen, a pretty, young female vamp who was good with other vamps that liked...well, vamps who liked other vamps, particularly of the same sex.

Gwen had not discovered much about Bronwyn Liddle, though she'd tried. The older vamp had not been interested in Gwen, but she must have liked something about her. What she'd given her was vague and ambiguous. After traveling with Rafe for almost a century, she'd killed him. She hadn't mentioned why. She'd been in Newark tracking down an old friend, a vamp named Ulric.

There was a note about Ulric. He had been linked to a vicious vampire called Troyer who'd been suspected of breeching federal law and killing humans. Troyer had never been caught. He'd died before anyone could verify the accusations. Ulric, too, was never heard from again. "Nice friends."

He sighed. It didn't take long to get to the end of the file. When he did, he found what he'd been looking for. *See Castus Vox.* He clicked the link. It didn't lead to the grand, detailed account he'd been hoping for. It led to a brief, vague blurb. Purported to have been present at the incident of 1954, in which twelve *Castus Vox* initiates were killed mysteriously in their Irish compound. The initiates did not appear to have died of vampire bites. At this time, there is no known cause of death.

Remy scowled. Where did they get this stuff? If someone had been left alive to tell who had been there, didn't they know something about it? It didn't seem like it. He scowled at the screen.

Known Associations: Cicely. See: Irish Sorceress.

He clicked the link. Now this was more like it. It seemed as though the Agency had taken greater pains to learn about the ancient witch. There was a photograph, though it appeared old and faded. She was a slender woman with large, green eyes and long, dark thick straight hair. She looked young, but she could not be young. She'd been around longer than Remy had been alive and probably would be long after he was dead. Her origins were unknown, but there had been stories about her in the areas around Cork and Munster for as long anyone remembered.

Her powers were professed to be vast and mysterious. According to the information the Agency's informants had gathered, Bronwyn had been seen with her on many occasions. The ancient witch favored the vampire. Rumor was she had imbued Bronwyn with powers no other vamp in the world possessed. The informant seemed hazy about what those powers were, exactly, but he seemed certain she was able to travel long distances without transportation. Remy frowned. It was not unheard of for a vampire to possess the ability to fly or shape shift.

If Bronwyn had powers, she was more dangerous than they had supposed.

There was nothing more. The informant confessed that his memory was a blank. He suspected the witch or her vampire friend had mesmerized him. After he'd met the witch in a pub in Cork, he'd woken up in a grungy alley with no memory of how he'd gotten there. He'd been clean and safe, but he was miles from the pub in which he'd started.

Remy sighed and leaned back in his chair. There was nothing in the report. He knew little more about her than when he'd started. He had more questions now than when Fallon had first envisioned her. If Bronwyn Liddle was in San Francisco, she had a reason, and it would probably end up being his problem. When mysterious vamps visited, it usually did.

He spun and rose from his chair. Fallon's visions usually meant something. Bronwyn Liddle might not be connected to the creature attacks, but she was important. Merek was the best place to start. He'd learned it was best to chase down Fallon's leads to the end, even when she was strung out on the elixir that heightened her senses and numbed the pain of her abilities for a little while. If Bronwyn didn't present a threat, she was off the hook

He turned back to his computer screen. He stared at it a moment. He hadn't been part of the *Castus Vox* for five years, since they'd thrown him out, but they were an old fashioned order. If they hadn't changed the database password...He typed in the IP address from memory. A strange sensation stole through him. It was anger and disappointment.

He'd made his own choices. He'd known the consequences.

Access Denied. Member is no longer active.

He sighed and dropped his head. His hands hovered over the glass keys of his flat virtual keyboard. A very faint black glow swirled around his fingers. He stared at his hands a long moment. Slowly, he lifted them from the keys.

He shot out of his chair and stormed out of the room.

* * *

It wasn't true that vampires could not see their reflection in a mirror. Gregor was grateful for the small courtesy super-nature had granted. It was important for a vampire to look one's best. He scoffed as he drew a hand carefully through his long, black hair. No one should have to look this good without being able to enjoy it.

He buttoned the sleeve of his black shirt and spun once in front of the mirror. He tossed his head and strode out of the room. When he saw Remy, he deflated. "Are you wearing that?"

Remy didn't even glance down at the jeans and white tee-shirt he wore. He rolled his eyes. "We're going to the Bleeding Orchid. We aren't going undercover. Are you wearing that?"

Gregor's smooth brow furrowed. He lifted his arms to indicate the opened black button-up shirt he wore tucked into black jeans so tight, they might have been painted on. His bare chest was smooth, sculpted and hairless. "What do you mean?"

Remy lifted an eyebrow. "Is there something you want to tell me?"

The dark-haired vampire stared at him with a bemused expression. "What?"

"You really want to go out like that?"

"What are you talking about? I always go out like this. What's wrong with it?"

"Aside from looking like the cover of one of those trashy romance novels we pretend not to know about, you look like a 90's teenage version of a vampire."

"This is a classic look!"

"For a vamp."

"Well, I am a vamp."

"That's not any reason to parade around with your fangs showing."

Gregor laughed and flashed Remy a sharp, toothy smile. "I'll try to keep them in my pants." He stepped aside as Skye strode into the lobby with his nose buried in a stack of paper.

Skye started and looked up. "Oh. You're on the way to the vamp bar to talk to Merek?"

"Yeah." Remy jerked his chin toward the file. "Anything interesting?"

"Yes. There have been similar attacks all over the country, but they've been more spread out. Missouri, Nebraska, Utah. They were all in small towns with no duty stations. Local law enforcement didn't call the nearest stations in, so they didn't investigate, but they archived the unusual deaths in case they might relate to a future case."

"Lucky us."

"Yes. I'm sending out a request to the local ME's to release the results on the autopsies and any trace evidence discovered on the bodies."

"Nice."

"I haven't found anything yet about any sort of hybrid monsters, though. This could be something totally new."

"You sound more gleeful than you ought to," Gregor said.

"Well, I like a challenge. I like new discoveries."

"Even if they're horrifying?" Remy asked.

Gregor snaked his tongue across his lower lip. "The more horrifying the better."

Skye grimaced slightly. "Yes. Well, off you go." He flicked his fingers dismissively at them and spun away with his nose still buried in his file. He paused and spun back around. "Remy, these attacks are our top priority."

Remy nodded. "Sure. We'll talk to Merek and see if what Bronwyn is doing here has something to do with them."

"If it doesn't, let it go. We can't rely on Fallon's visions right now. Not in her condition. We need to focus on the attacks and make the deaths stop. We can worry about a potential hostile later."

"Sure."

Skye lifted a disdainful eyebrow in Gregor's direction. "And Greg, don't let anyone know you work for us. I don't want the Agency mistaken for a Harlequin novel."

* * *

The streets outside the Bleeding Orchid vampire bar in Soma were cheerful and noisy. Music pounded out into the streets from the open doors of the clubs, and people gathered in the streets outside, talking and laughing. They looked as though they hadn't a care in the world. They certainly didn't look as though they knew there was a cluster of vampires and other paranormals hanging out in the dark, basement bar around the corner in the alley, waiting for a willing victim to wander in.

"This always seemed like an odd place for a vamp bar," Remy remarked, striding through the crowds toward the alley entrance over which a wooden sign with a hand-painted purple orchid bled a single drop like a tear.

He ignored the interested eyes he and Gregor drew as they passed. He had the uncomfortable feeling they were being mistaken as a couple. Remy took a step away from him, just in case. Gregor, on the other hand, seemed to enjoy the attention. He tossed his dark, wavy hair and smiled alluringly around.

There was one thing that would never change. It was no wonder Hollywood romanticized vampires. No one would ever want to have their blood drained if not for all the sexy vampires striding around making it look so appealing.

There was a bounce in Gregor's step as they descended the stairs to the Bleeding Orchid. At least this aspect of the vamp bar was typical. They sure liked being underground. It was because vampires didn't necessarily sleep during the day. They just had to stay indoors. Spending the daylight hours drinking in a basement bar was one way to wile away those lonely, sleepless days.

Remy expected dark, moody music, smoke, blood red lights and darkly-clothed people writhing obscenely upon each other when they pushed open the heavy wooden door. Instead, upbeat pop music was playing, and everyone—even the oldest, most weathered-looking vamps--was bobbing their heads in time. There were a few people dancing in a small space in the far corner of the room. They all looked happy, not brooding.

It didn't look anything like a vamp bar until Remy caught sight of the small clusters of couples ensconced in dark corners, bent over each other's necks or between their legs. He even saw a young, pretty Asian girl spread open to a thin male vampire, who seemed to be sucking her blood from her inner thigh. A beautiful women sucked on her neck, gently stroking her face and her exposed breasts. The young girl had a look of pure, shameless ecstasy on her face. They were not unique.

The Bleeding Orchid served liquor. It was a bring your own blood kind of place.

Gregor slunk to the bar like a large jungle cat stalking its prey. He ordered red wine with a splash of Chambord. Remy asked for a bourbon and Coke and rolled his eyes at his partner. He liked Gregor a lot better when he was acting like a normal person and not the 1990's Hollywood goth version of a vamp. Now he swiveled his hips to the music in a strange, sinuous slither.

A very pretty human girl approached them as though his dance was an irresistible mating call. She had very bright red hair and large, stunning blue eyes. She was too thin for Remy's taste. Her collar bone jutted out over the top of her low cut black dress. He preferred healthy, buxom women. Gregor didn't seem to mind her slight figure. His smile was sensual and predatory, and she pressed against him, laying her palm on his bare chest.

No words passed between them. Gregor's eyes flashed up at Remy. Remy rolled his eyes. "Make it quick." His voice was so quiet, only Gregor's superior vamp hearing could pick it up--and maybe a few dozen other vamps in the immediate area. "And be careful. She looks like an ounce too much will kill her."

It was a necessary fact of life that Gregor had to feed. As long as he did so within the confines of the law--that is, he took willing donors and didn't kill anyone--the Agency looked the other way. They liked to pretend their vampires were abstinent. Remy had expected to lose Gregor the moment they strode into the bar. In fact, he'd lasted longer than usual.

Being a human in a vamp bar is like being catnip in a kitten kennel. Remy lifted his glass to his lips. He blinked, and when he opened his eyes, a tall, ethereally beautiful woman with long, blonde hair stood before him. His eyes dropped to the full, milky white cleavage above the low décolletage of the sheer, flowing white dress. She wasn't wearing a bra, and her pert, pale pink nipples strained against the fabric. She smiled when she caught the direction of his gaze and pressed her breasts against his chest. Her teeth were already sharpening.

She slithered against him. She lifted her thigh to rub gently against his crotch. Arousal pulse through him and tightened his cock. "Come here often?"

"Yeah. When I'm working." He flashed his badge in her face.

She reacted exactly as he expected. She recoiled as though he'd burned her. She bared her teeth. "Agency?"

"That's right."

She hissed softly.

"I'm looking for Merek. Is he here?"

She glared at him for a split second. Then her lovely elfin features smoothed. "He's here." She lifted a single eyebrow. "I would be willing to show you. For a small fee."

She was beside him before he saw her move. Her hand slid from his neck down to his chest and then cupped his groin, squeezing slightly and rolling his testicles in her hand. Her silky smooth breasts brushed against his chest. She breathed a husky chuckle in his ear as his cock went rigid.

He pressed a hand to her chest. She inhaled sharply and arched her back to offer her breasts to his palm. He didn't touch them. Instead, he shoved her gently away. "No thanks. I'm not into being dinner."

She didn't seem discouraged. She moved back against him. Her hand slid into his waistband, and her tongue flicked out to drag across the shell of his ear. She drew her hand up the length of his cock and squeezed the engorged head with more strength than necessary. Her palm and fingers was ice cold. If it had been warm, he would have come in her hand in front of all these vampires. They were already circling around as though they smelled his arousal. "I don't always use my teeth." Her breath was icy. "Sometimes I just use my tongue."

He caught her wrists and extricated himself from the chill of her clutches. "I'm working. Maybe some other time."

An angry expression crossed her features for a split second, and then she was gone, disappearing into the crowd as quickly as she'd appeared. He never even got her name. He didn't really want it. He didn't come to these bars to pick up vamp women. He came because there wasn't anywhere else to find Merek.

Remy could find Merek on his own, but the vamp seemed to prefer to deal with other vamps, even if he did work with the Agency from time to time. Despite his ridiculous clothes and vampire romance novel facade, Gregor was good at his job, and Remy could count on him. Before Remy had begun his second bourbon and Coke, Gregor appeared at his side looked rosy and satisfied. Remy wondered if he'd had sex as well as blood, then decided he didn't want to know. If he had, it probably hadn't been that good. He'd only been gone a few minutes.

Of course, vampires could move very quickly. They might only need a few minutes to blow their sex partners' minds. Remy wouldn't know.

Gregor jerked his head. "Merek's over there."

'Other there' was a corner so clouded with smoke, Remy coughed as he stepped into the acrid fog. They didn't glimpse Merek through the smoke until they had bumped into his table. Merek had been in his mid-thirties when he'd been vamped. He looked and spoke as though he'd come from the Middle East or the Mediterranean, but he'd never revealed the secret of his origin or his vampire age. He had a mop of thick, curly dark hair. His dark eyes were large and slanted. His narrow, unlined, intelligent face looked as though it had once been tan but the color had been drained from it.

He was good looking. Most vamps were good-looking, even if they'd been plain in real life. This quality might have been part of the change from human to vampire; part of the rebirth and regeneration of cells by a supernatural force. It might have just been another element of their ability to mesmerize the humans around them The beauty, sensuality, allure they projected to attract their prey.

Merek snuffed out his cigarette and smiled up at them. "Ah. The Agency. I did expect to see you around here eventually." He cupped his palm around his lighter as he lit another cigarette. He offered one to Gregor.

Remy lifted an eyebrow. "Why?"

"I have heard there are a lot of things going on around town."

"Such as?"

"There's a new kind of killer in town, isn't there?"

"You heard that? You know about the attacks?"

Merek blinked. For a moment, there was confusion in his eyes, as though the word didn't quite sit right with him. "This doesn't seem like your kind of work. We have people on our side for this."

Remy frowned. "What are you talking about?"

"Come on. I know you've only been inside for five years, but you know about our people. There are paranormals who do what you do, keep it out of the public eye." He smiled a toothy smile. "They're not government sanctioned, but they're often more effective."

Remy smirked slightly. "I'm pretty sure I'm not supposed to know about that or I might have to do something about it."

"I'll let you just look the other way, then."

"So you know about the creature attacks?" Gregor asked, puffing out a series of perfect, effortless smoke rings with each word.

"You mean the attacks on creatures? We prefer the term paranormals, Greg. You've been inside too long."

"No. The attacks by creatures. New creatures. Part wolf, part vamp and some kind of demon."

Merek stared at him in silent surprise for a split second. "I haven't heard about that."

Remy sighed. Gregor frowned. "What are you talking about?" he asked.

"The attacks on our kind. Lately there have been an unusual number of vamps disappearing off the streets and out of their nests."

The agents exchanged a glance. "Disappearing? "

"Yeah. We had some witnesses who claimed one minute a vamp was beside them and the next, they were just gone."

"No idea what's happening to them? "

"It's like something is moving so quickly, it can grab them and take off with them before even one of us notices."

Gregor frowned. "That's very unusual."

"Yes. And worrisome, as you might imagine."

"Are they being staked?"

Merek shook his head. "There's no way to know, but there isn't any of the evidence you normally find—a big pile of ash or left over clothing and jewelry. They are disappearing completely."

"How come we didn't know about this?"

Merek shrugged. "It's not exactly the sort of thing we report to the police and the newspapers, is it? We clean it up quietly. No one misses the vamps because they aren't officially recognized citizens, and we disappear and move around all the time."

Remy scowled. "We need to get better informants. We haven't heard from our guy in a long time."

Merek lifted his eyebrows. "Odo? He's gone."

"What do you mean 'he's gone?'"

"He's missing. He's been missing a couple weeks." Merek leaned back in his chair and lit another cigarette. "He might have left town when the disappearances started, or he might have been one of the victims."

"Hm."

Merek gave Gregor a sharp, narrow look. "Maybe if you spent more time with your kind and less with the government, you would know more about our world." He smirked slightly. "And you could be dressed more like a modern vamp than an old relic, Gregor. Honestly."

This did not seem to offend the Italian vamp, but Gregor looked around as though he missed living full-time as a vampire. He didn't reply.

"You're telling me some kind of patchwork creature is attacking people?"

"Yes. The police have discovered evidence of two different kinds of wolves, a vampire and what indicates some sort of demon."

"They usually don't run around together."

"No. They aren't. There seems to only be one creature that's all of them at once. It's possible someone is making creatures. Maybe they're the one snatching the vamps. "

Merek looked appalled. "Splicing us with dogs? Disgusting. The smell alone..."

Remy lifted his hand. "So you've never heard of anyone who can do that sort of thing?"

"I've never heard of anyone so sick in my life, and I have seen a lot of depraved things."

Remy sat back in his chair. He wasn't sure if Merek's attacks were related to his creature, but he wondered how things had gotten so out of hand before they'd noticed anything was wrong. He frowned. They'd become too reliant on Fallon's visions for guidance, and she was spiraling steadily downward. He sighed. "If you hear anything about our creature, let us know."

"Sure." Merek's expression was closed, and Remy suspected they he wouldn't, not without a little persuasion. That could be arranged.

Gregor fixed him with a sharp, piercing gaze. "What do you know about a vampire named Bronwyn Liddle?"

Merek's eyebrows shot up in surprise. He narrowed his eyes, and then his face slipped into a blank mask. "I have met her."

"Do you know why she's in town?"

Merek seemed to consider this a long moment. "A visit? San Francisco is beautiful this time of year. It attracts all sorts."

"Don't waste our time," Remy barked. "We aren't stupid and neither are you. We know you know her, and we know you know what she's doing here."

"What are you interested in her for? Is it something to do with your creature attacks?" He sounded blasé, but his voice was pitched a slight octave higher. He was hiding something.

"We're not sure." Remy stared at him. "We were hoping you might be able to help us with that."

Merek glanced between them with a calculating expression. He seemed to decide it was pointless to hold out, but he didn't give the impression he wanted to talk about her. "Wyn is complicated. No one really knows why she does anything."

"Merek, just tell us if we should be on the lookout for her."

He hesitated. "I'm not sure exactly how to answer that."

Remy rolled his eyes. "Is she a good guy or a bad guy?"

"She's not either. She has her own code; she follows her own rules."

Remy scowled at him as though he was being purposely ambiguous. "Why is she here?"

The old vampire lit another cigarette and considered the question. "She has business."

"And here I thought we were all getting along. Now you're going to belt up and make us unhappy?"

Merek's dark eyes flicked to him nervously. He tended to remain on the Agency's good side; it made his and everyone else's lives easier. Just now, though, he was not being very cooperative. "There are worse things than risking your happiness, St. John." His tone was low.

Remy lifted an eyebrow. "Is that loyalty or fear, Merek?"

Merek scowled. "I don't have to tell you anything. Wyn hasn't done anything wrong, and this is harassment. I already told you more than I have to. I've been very cooperative. Don't push things too far."

Remy sighed and lifted his hands in surrender. "All right, all right. We're still friends."

Merek relaxed and nodded, but his jaw was still rigid. His eyes flashed. He stared at the stack of ten dollar bills Remy pushed across the table: his usual fee for informing to the Agency. When Remy lifted his hand, Merek pushed the money back at him. "Consider it my civic duty. You help find out who is killing our people, I'll consider it a wash."

Remy sat back in his chair. "Right. Thanks, Merek." They did not offer their hands for him to shake as they rose.

Merek flicked his fingers at them in dismissal.

Gregor didn't seem to want to leave the Bleeding Orchid. Remy stepped out into the cool night air without waiting for him. He was staring at the sky when Gregor followed seconds later, looking slightly disappointed. "Do you think the vamp attacks have anything to do with the creatures?" He didn't even glance at Gregor.

Gregor shrugged. "It seems as though there are too many things happening at once for them to be unrelated. Not to mention this Bronwyn Liddle. She's here for a reason. People are talking about it."

"What are they saying?"

"I just hear her name murmured through the crowd. No one seems to know anything, but they know she's here. Everyone seems to be waiting for something. I've never seen Merek so upset before." He lifted an eyebrow. "Do you think they're involved?"

Remy shrugged. "How the hell would I know? I think it's something else, though. I think he's afraid of her. I want to find her and figure out what she's doing here. Something tells me she has something to do with all this."

Gregor glanced at him. "Why would she? Merek didn't even know about the creature attacks. Bronwyn probably has nothing to do with it."

Remy shook his head. "I just have this feeling they're related. I think she might be here to stop the vamp attacks Merek mentioned."

"She's a vigilante."

"Maybe. Or she has some personal motivations."

Gregor nodded. "I'll talk to the vamps and see what I can find out about the disappearances. They might know more about Bronwyn Liddle than they're admitting around you."

Remy nodded. "Speaking of that...what the hell happened to Odo? And how come no one even noticed he was missing?"

* * *

Skye sighed up at his computer monitor. "This is much worse than we thought."

"Yeah." Remy frowned and perched on the edge of the conference table. "We've got vamps being attacked, a hybrid creature attacking humans and a centuries old vamp running around loose in the city that everyone, including Merek seems to be afraid of."

"So what do we do?" Fallon asked.

"We have to sort out what is important." Skye's pale eyes pierced Remy as though he could read his thoughts. Remy had wondered from time to time if he actually could. "You've got a bee in your bonnet over this vampress, but none of this connects back to her."

"Not yet, anyway." Remy crossed his arms over his chest. "None of it connects to anyone. That doesn't mean they aren't involved. Did you hear anything from oversight?"

"Not much. There are a few biologists who might turn out to be suspects, but none of them are known to be in the area. That doesn't mean they aren't."

"It's worth looking into. Who have we got?" Remy sat down at his station to peer up at his screen. The team took their places in the semi-circle around the laboratory and waited for Skye to send the biologists' files to their screens.

"It sounds like our suspect is traveling," Skye announced as he punched up the files on his virtual keyboard. "He's left a trail of bodies across the country."

A series of photos and profiles appeared on their screen. They all skimmed through them cursorily. "Why these guys?" Noah asked.

"They all have some kind of history of biological tampering or delving in supernatural science. Some of them were our guys; others have just been flagged by the Agency. It doesn't mean they're our only suspects; just the ones we know about right now."

Fallon bobbed her head. "I will see if I can lock these guys down or figure out if they're traveling or unaccounted for."

"What about the vampire disappearances?" Gregor asked in a slightly sullen voice.

"Odo is missing," Skye confirmed. "I tried to track him down when I received your intel. There was no response from him."

"He could be one of the taken vamps," Remy mused. "Or he might have just taken off. He was always a damn coward, even if he was useful sometimes."

Skye nodded. "It's not unusual for us to lose an asset."

"No, but it's a little coincidental, under the circumstances."

"Yes, I agree."

"So how do we track down Bronwyn Liddle?" Noah asked, spinning around in his chair. He preferred action to sorting through personnel files.

"We could use the usual way," Remy said. "But I don't think our instruments will be much help."

"We don't know anything about her. There's nothing in her history that mentions San Francisco. I'm not sure where she would be," Gregor put in.

"We could check the property records," Noah suggested. "A lot of the times the older vamps have enough disposable cash to just buy a place wherever they go."

"Lucky jerks," Gregor complained. He worked because he still needed the money. He'd only been alive since the late thirties. He'd been born and raised in Rome. He claimed to have been an extra in the movie *Roman Holiday*. Remy suspected he was telling the truth, but he hadn't bothered to check. Gregor hadn't ever made it as an actor, even though he was a pretty good one.

"Not so lucky," Noah muttered. "They still have to suck blood to survive like every poor vamp."

"It could be worse," Remy said. "Gregor seems to enjoy it all right."

"They all enjoy it. It's part of the bloodlust thing they're reborn with."

"I'm still in the room. I can hear you."

"You could hear us even if you weren't in the room, Greg."

"I'm checking property records for Bronwyn Liddle or some derivative now," Fallon put in.

"Check the hotels and the usual places," Skye added.

She rolled her eyes as though this was highly insulting.

"If worse comes to worse," Gregor said slyly, "we can always hang out in Soma until she shows herself. It will be like an old-fashioned stake out."

"Man," Noah complained. "I hate stake outs so much, I'm not even going to take advantage of that awesome punning opportunity."

Remy rolled his eyes. "We appreciate that."

Noah turned his head to looked at Fallon. She typed furiously on her glass keyboard. Her fingernails looked short and raw, as though she'd been gnawing them. There were dark circles under her eyes. "Fallon, you look tired. You should rest. I can do the computer work." His voice was soft and gentle. She cut him a sideways scowl. "I can search databases as well as anyone else."

She shook her head. "No. I just need some coffee. People are dying. You should be patrolling the streets in case the creature attacks again."

"The attacks are occurring at random," Skye explained. "All within a four week period. One happened, a few days went by, there was another, and then it was about two weeks before the next. There's no way to form a pattern. We don't know if it will be days or weeks before the next one."

"Have you got an area we can canvas?" Remy asked. "It might help us pin down an area the suspect's holed up."

Fallon nodded. "I can get the computer to run a schematic." Her fingers flew over the virtual keyboard. She pointed to her monitor as points appeared on a topographical map of the city. "It seems to be happening within about a five block radius in the Tenderloin."

"How about the vamp attacks?"

"I had one of Merek's people send the locations of the killings--if they are killings," Gregor said. He frowned at Remy. "You must have pissed him off, Rem. He won't even talk to me now. I had to talk to his flunky, Justine. She hates me."

Remy flicked his hand dismissively. "He's being a pussy baby boy about Bronwyn Liddle."

Fall snorted. "Well, some people don't like to sell out their friends." She glared at him. "Some people have friends."

Remy ignored this. "Do the areas of the attacks coincide?"

"Not really. The vamp attacks are mostly in areas the vamps hang out. There's no real relation to the creature attacks zones, but we're talking about totally different creatures with totally different prey."

"Yeah," Noah said thoughtfully. "It makes sense the vamps are being hunted where they are, but the Tenderloin...if the attacks are within a small area, it's probably safe to assume it's hunting near home. It hasn't spread out. The creature's probably being held in a single location."

"Like a lab where they're splicing things," Gregor muttered sullenly.

Noah grinned. "Or an island."

"There's no island, Noah," Remy snapped.

"Okay, so get out there and patrol this five miles," Skye said.

"Great." Noah hopped to his feet. "I'm on it."

Skye sighed. "I'm going to call around and see if anyone has seen Odo. It would be nice to know what he knows about the vamp attacks—"

"If he isn't already a victim of one," Gregor interrupted.

Skye went on as if he hadn't. "He'll know if the paranormal community has any suspects."

None of them were paying attention to him anymore. Noah was already strapping weapons to his belt and over his shoulder. He was an action man, and he couldn't wait to get out of research duty, no matter how gallant he was toward Fallon. Remy and Fallon were peering at their screens as though they were the most fascinating things in the world.

Remy didn't much care for research either, but he thought his time was better spent searching the property records than patrolling for a creature that may or may not appear. There was a good chance Bronwyn Liddle wasn't staying at a hotel or renting a house. A lot of vamps were good at discovering old empty cathedrals and crypts—any creepy place in the city. They liked to hide. He didn't really expect to find anything, but it was better to try before giving up. If he had to, he would spend the entire night in Soma waiting for her to appear. He hoped Merek hadn't tipped her off.

When vamps were taking up temporary residence in San Francisco and preferred clean, modern accommodations to dank, dreary tombs, they stayed at the After Dark Hotel. It didn't look like a luxury hotel from the outside. In fact, it looked a lot like an old, abandoned building. There were no windows on the guest floors; it was the only light-tight high rise hotel in the Bay Area, and it was hard to get in to. It was a vamps only hotel. If a human stumbled in or attempted to book reservations, they were politely informed the hotel had no vacancy.

He knew one of the managers there. He strode out of the lab and punched up her number on his cell phone. He paced the hallway as he waited for her to answer.

"Maggie Jaqueway."

"Maggie, it's Remy St. John."

There was a tiny intake of breath on the other end of the line. She sounded like she was smiling when she spoke again. "Hello, Remy. I assume you want something?"

"Yeah. Sorry, Maggie."

"She sighed. "I might have known. It's the only reason you ever call. I'm used to it by now. What is it, then?"

He felt a little guilty, but if he called just to talk to every asset, he'd never have time to work. "Have you got a record for a new vamp staying there by the name of Bronwyn Liddle?"

She didn't reply immediately. He heard the keys tapping on her keyboard. "No. No vampire by that name is registered."

"Any new arrivals?"

Maggie huffed. "They're coming and going so fast, they aren't even paying their bills."

He lifted his eyebrows. "Really? What's that mean?"

"We've had a lot of walk-outs lately. It's not typical. Vampires usually pay up no problem."

"Do you think something is happening to them?"

"Maybe. I've been hearing things around here. Vamps are disappearing in the city." She sounded slightly amused as she added, "They seem to think it's your people."

"What? They think the Agency is behind it?"

"Well, they always suspect the government when something like this happens, don't they? Anyway, you aren't doing anything to stop it, are you? That's just as bad."

He frowned. "We're trying. I need to find Bronwyn Liddle."

"Has she got something to do with it?"

"I don't know, but I think she might have information that could help us."

Maggie sighed. "All right. A lot of vamps like to use aliases. What's she look like?"

"Long red hair, dark eyes. Pretty."

"Yeah, they're all pretty. "

"I don't know much about her. I've never seen her in person. I haven't even seen a photograph; just a sketch. It might not even be accurate."

"That's helpful."

"Yeah."

"If she comes in, should I tell her you're looking for her?"

"No. Call me instead. Any hour of the day."

"Right. It was nice talking to you, Rem. Maybe next time you'll call for other reasons."

"I will, Maggie."

She was smiling again. He could hear it in her voice. "No, you won't."

He smiled a little and snapped the phone shut. No, he probably wouldn't. His phone vibrated in his hand, and he stared down at it in surprise. Gregor. He peeked his head into the lab. Gregor wasn't there.

"Where's Greg?"

Fallon and Skye looked up at him in surprise. "He left. Said he was going to Soma to do some recon."

"How did I not notice?"

Fallon shrugged. "He moves fast?"

Remy sighed ducked back out into the hall to answer the call. "Yeah, Greg."

"Remy."

"You've been gone five seconds. Are you in trouble already?"

Gregor scoffed. "I've learned some things."

"Already?"

"Yes."

"Okay."

"Some of the vampires seem to think the others are being attacked during the day and taken away."

"Yeah. We heard about this already."

"As far as we can tell, no one's been killed yet."

"You think they might be alive somewhere?"

"Maybe. No one knows. They're taken from the streets, their homes or their nests and never seen again."

"It sounds like they might be taken from After Dark, as well. Maggie said a lot of them have been disappearing before paying their bills."

"That doesn't surprise me. Whoever is taking them is very fast."

"So no one's seen anything?"

"No. Aside from the few times someone noticed them disappear from right beside them, the kidnapper is taking them one by one from their homes. They're not ambushing nests and killing or taking everyone inside at once. It's a slow, steady stream of disappearances. There are about four or five a week for the last couple months. Sometimes more"

"That doesn't sound like an epidemic. What about the others?"

"Some of them took off. A few of them told someone before they left. The rest just left town without a word. Word on the streets is it's safer not to be San Francisco right now."

"So, who's taking them?"

"Well, I hate to jump to conclusions here, Rem, but if someone is splicing creatures together, it might be they need creatures to experiment on."

"Huh. But vamps aren't the only creatures being spliced."

"Yeah. We should ask around the werewolf packs and see if they're missing any of their people, as well. We might have heard about that on the news. They're actually considered people most of the time. They live a lot easier out in the open."

He sounded a little bitter. Remy thought about it. "I'll check it out. I'll let you know if I learn anything. Have you heard anything about Bronwyn Liddle?"

"Yeah. A lot, actually."

"Seriously, how long have you been gone?"

"I'm a vampire. We move fast."

"What have you heard?"

"Not a lot that makes any sort of sense. Everyone seems to have some story to tell about her, but none of them seem very likely to be true."

"What sort of stories?"

"She's like a boogeyman legend to vamps. She can walk in daylight, shape-shift, fly--"

"Fly?"

"Yeah, well, you know how vamps are about their legends."

"So what is she doing here?"

"No one knows, but they're scared of her. When Bronwyn Liddle comes to town, someone dies."

"So, she's a killer."

"Yes, but I don't think she murders people."

"Well, what's that mean, then?"

"I think maybe she's a vigilante."

"Oh, god, not one of those. A vamp hunting their own kind?"

"You never know. She killed her sire. Maybe she's the one snatching the vamps. They did say the person moved fast and was never seen. Someone who can fly and shape shift could probably easily snatch a vamp off the street and take off with them."

Remy sighed. "So she's killing them out of some twisted sense of justice?"

"It could be."

"She might actually be able to do those things."

Gregor paused for a split second. "Cicely."

"Right. She's a powerful sorceress. If she's figured out the secret to eternal life, maybe she can give a vamp a spell to fly or shape shift. You've never met a vamp who could do it?"

He couldn't see Gregor's face, but he was sure the old vamp was scowling. "Nah. Except Dracula, and he isn't real. He was just some punk kid telling tales."

"So do we consider her hostile or not?"

Gregor thought about this. "I'm not sure. I wouldn't want to be meet her in a dark alley, but I'm not sure she's a threat to us. She's just very dangerous."

"Okay. Do any of your people know where to find her?"

"No one knows where she's staying or what she's up to, but she's been around the Orchid a few times to talk to Merek."

"I knew he was holding out."

"Don't blame him. If what I've heard is true, she can mesmerize any of us."

"Ah. Great. Even better."

"So, what's the plan, boss?"

"We need to talk to the were pack leaders."

"Oh, no. Not me. You remember what happened last time. I do not play well with dogs."

"Fine. I'll call Seth and see if he's heard anything. I think we're on speaking terms since I sprung his pack-mate from jail during the full moon before the police sergeant saw him change. He always knows what's going on with the other packs."

"I'll stick around here and see if our vampress shows up. It's still early. I might hear more about the disappearances. You know how these places are."

"Yeah. Full of willing women. Remember you're on business, not pleasure."

"I am a professional, Remy. I highly resent your implication."

"Yeah, yeah. Just keep your fangs to yourself. I haven't got time to pull you out if you pick up an elder's midnight snack again."

"God. You are so negative all the time. You never let anything go, do you?"

CHAPTER THREE

Remy hated being cooped up in the office while Gregor and Noah were out prowling the streets in search of rogue vampires and patchwork monsters. He paced the small space of his private room on the third floor. His laptop screen was blank. He paused the peer down at the small, overgrown courtyard below the window. When it had been a government library, the garden had been well-tended. It was neglected now. It was a shame. It had once boasted the most magnificent roses in the neighborhood.

Dark energy swirled on the edge of his vision, distracting him from the mossy stone fountain and the gnarled tangle of thorny, flowerless bushes. He lifted his hands. They shook slightly. Darkness shot from his fingertips like mist and dissipated in the air around them.

He needed to sleep. If he didn't sleep soon, the energy would turn his eyes to black and engulf him like Merek's cloud of smoke. He would black out, and then he would lose control of himself. There was no way to know what he would do then. It wouldn't be good.

Fallon wasn't the only one with problems. She was right; he had no room to talk.

He flipped open his cell phone and punched up a number. Despite the lateness of the hour, it rang only twice before the low, gruff voice answered, "What?"

Seth was still awake. The paranormals were usually awake, even in the earliest hours of morning. "It's Remy."

There was silence for a split second. "What's up, Rem?" He sounded nervous, as though he was bracing himself for bad news.

"You sound like something's wrong."

"Yeah. Something is."

"Let me guess. Your people are going missing one by one. Snatched right from the streets."

Seth's breath hissed out. "Yeah."

"How many?"

"Three of my pack, more from others."

Remy scowled. "How come no one tells us about this stuff?"

"How come you don't already know? You're supposed to know everything."

"We're falling down on the job these days, apparently. One of our assets is missing."

"There's something bad in town, man, if they can take our kinds off the streets."

Remy considered. He sighed. "How about a centuries old vamp who can shape shift and fly?"

Seth chuckled dryly. "Yeah, that would do it. You know one of those?"

He didn't sound as though he expected Remy's reply. "Not yet. I think I'm about to meet her."

"Vamps can't actually do that, you know."

Remy thought about this. "No, not so far as we know about, but I'm beginning to realize there are a lot of things I don't know about."

"That's a little worrying."

"I know. You ever heard of a vamp called Bronwyn Liddle?"

There was a soft, low growling noise from the other end of the line, as though Seth was snarling from the back of his throat. "Yeah. I've heard of her."

"You know her?"

"I've never met her. I heard she killed a were a few years ago in Vancouver."

"Really. You got any details on that?"

"No, not really. I just know she killed one of our people."

"They say when she comes to town, someone dies."

"Sounds about right."

"All I can find out about her is people die when she's around."

Seth paused. "If you're thinking about going after her, you'd better be careful. I hear she has tricks no one has seen before."

"Yeah. I've heard the same things. I'm not sure if I believe it."

"It's safer to believe it. I don't care much for the Agency, but you're all right. Don't die."

Remy snorted.

"You find out who's taking my people, give me a call. If you need back up muscle, you know where to find me."

Remy smiled. "Yeah. Thanks, Seth. And thanks for the information."

"Sure."

Remy snapped the phone shut and sat down on the edge of his bed. He sighed, and then he fell back on the mattress. He didn't bother to remove his clothes or boots. Dark magic shimmered around him. It blurred his vision until the blackness swallowed him and he passed out.

* * *

An unidentified commotion from the lobby jolted him awake. Loud voices. A crash? He shot up off the bed and checked his watch. 4 a.m. He'd only been asleep an hour. It was still dark outside his window. He sighed. He could sleep when the sun rose. At least most of his work happened in the darkness.

He looked down at his hands. The dark energy still clung to his flesh like cobwebs. He closed his eyes and concentrated. When he looked down again, his hands were normal. The brief nap had strengthened him. He could contain himself for a little while longer. He felt better. He felt as though the tension roiling around inside him was calm for the moment. It wouldn't last. Soon, it would be almost impossible to control.

He scrubbed his hands down the sides of his face. He shook his head a little as if to clear it, and then he strode quickly from his bedroom and bounded down the stairs to the lobby.

It had been Noah who'd awakened him. The lobby door hung open as though he hadn't been able to secure it properly. It creaked in the early morning breeze. Noah was still on his feet, but it looked as though the effort to stand were as painful as the slashes on his face. Blood still oozed from the wounds. His eyes were blackened. He looked as though he'd gone several rounds with a boxer who was wearing claws rather than gloves. He held his ribs as if they were broken. His clothes were shredded.

"Hey, man!" Remy said, rushing toward him.

Fallon flew into the lobby. She was faster than Remy. She caught Noah as he fell to his knees. He clutched at her, and she struggled for a moment under his weight. "Okay. Come on, Noah. Skye can fix you up." She glanced up at Remy with a haunted expression. "I can't get him in there on my own."

Skye was waiting in the ritual lab on the bottom floor when Remy and Fallon hoisted Noah inside. The ritual lab had once been the old books storage room, and it still held the must of ancient, moth-eaten texts. Skye had a few ancient texts of his own. They were kept in cases along the stark, cement walls. The center of the room had been cleared to make room for a perfect circle of quartz crystal. There was nothing inside the crystal barrier but smooth, polished marble floor. The walls of the room were stacked up with tables that held a collection of colored crystals, vials of foul and sweet smelling liquids, bottles of herbs, amulets, knives, tiny marble bowls and polished glass discs.

Remy felt the dark energy inside him surge, as though it was desperate for release. He hated being in the ritual lab. It got his mojo running a little more than he liked. He took a deep, steadying breath and helped Fallon lower Noah into the center of the crystal circle.

Skye shooed Fallon and Remy away and bent to examine Noah. The soldier did not speak. Remy was surprised he'd made it home on his own in his condition. Fallon took one of the chairs along the wall and leaned her elbows on her knees. "What happened, Noah?" she asked anxiously.

Skye glared at her as he strode toward the cases of books. "Don't try to talk, Noah. Step away from him, Remy." He unlocked a case housing a thick, crumbling tome that looked as though the cover had once been purple silk but was now discolored and rough to the touch. The pages felt as though they might turn to dust at any moment. Skye handled it carelessly, however. It didn't seem injured.

They watched silently as Skye paged swiftly through the book. He slapped his hand down on the page he'd been looking for. His eyes skimmed the words so rapidly, they seemed not to even be moving behind his glasses. He placed the book on a long, narrow marble table and selected a series of vials and bottles.

His lips moved in a low, incomprehensible murmur. Filmy, white energy swirled around him like translucent, pliable cobwebs. He tossed herbs and splashed water on Noah in seemingly random patterns. He did not speak or acknowledge any of them. It went on for several moments. Noah didn't move. Remy sighed and leaned against the wall. Fallon seemed to be watching closely, though Remy doubted she could understand what was happening.

Finally, Skye set down the bottles and vials. He stood back and looked at Noah smugly, as if to admire his handiwork.

Suddenly, Noah's body convulsed. A haze of pure white energy surrounded him. For several moments, the room was completely silent. Then the fog around

Noah dissipated. He rose to his feet. His wounds weren't gone, but they looked as though he'd had weeks to heal. He patted his chest and face. He grinned. "Thanks, Skye."

Skye inclined his head modestly. Remy vaulted off the wall and strode toward Noah. "So what happened? Did you see the monster?"

"Yeah." Noah frowned. The bruises under his eyes and on his forehead were turning an awful yellow. Remy fought the urge to press on them to discover if they were still tender. They probably were. "Sort of. While I was patrolling, I saw a huge shadow in an alley. I went in and saw something bending over a vagrant. I shot at it. It turned and came after me instead. It ran right at me."

"So?" Remy demanded. "Did you see what it looked like?"

"It was dark, and it was huge. I just saw fur and scales and teeth."

"Was it humanoid?" Skye asked.

"Yeah. A bit. It was shaped like a man. It seemed to have a man's face, but there was so much fur and scales all over it--all in random patches--I couldn't see enough to get an ID."

"So that's our monster."

Noah scowled. "I like chicken cows better."

"Seriously, dude. Move on."

"So, we're right about the monsters," Skye mused. "Were you able to see where it went?"

He looked a little put out by this. "No. It mauled me, man. You saw the state of me."

"Did it bite you?"

"Nah. It snapped at me a bit, but I didn't let it get me. It had a long, forked tongue. I was afraid it was venomous. I cut it off."

"You cut off his tongue?"

"Well, it was coming at me! Anyway, it probably just grew back. When I did it, it jumped off me and ran."

Skye lifted his eyebrows. "I don't suppose you have the tongue?"

"No. I tried to grab it, but it just disintegrated in my hands."

"Damn." Remy cursed.

"Did you follow it?"

"Yeah. I tried. It was so fast, I lost it a couple streets over."

They all considered this. "So we've got a monster," Fallon said with a sigh.

"A new monster," Remy added.

"It seemed a little weird." Noah looked around at them with a frown. "It seemed sad."

"Sad?" Fallon said.

"You would be too if you were made from intelligent creatures. They're probably aware of what's been done to them," Skye said darkly.

"I don't think it was meant to get out onto the streets," Noah said thoughtfully. "I think whoever is making the monsters means to keep them locked up. It might be escaping."

"It doesn't really manner," Fallon snapped. "Even if his intention isn't to unleash it on the world, it doesn't mean he's not still doing something evil by creating them."

"So let's stop him then," Remy said.

"Guys," Noah said in a low, ominous sort of voice. "Has it occurred to anyone else that there have been a lot of creatures taken from the streets? It might not be only the one monster."

They all turned to look at him as the horror dawned on them. "There might be an army of these things?" Fallon asked.

"Who knows how far he's come in the process of building them," Skye added.

"Oh, god. What do you think he wants to do with them?"

"No idea. Maybe keep them like a horror movie menagerie or eventually unleash them on the world when they're ready."

"Oh, that sounds really bad," Remy muttered.

"I know, right?"

Gregor swept into the room like a dark, silent shadow. His dark eyes glittered in exhilaration. "So what's going on, then?" He paused and sniffed the air. "What's happened? I smell blood."

"Noah met the creature in a dark alley."

Gregor looked at Noah in interest. "You don't look too bad. How's he look?"

"Skye patched me up. I didn't come off too well."

"So did you bag it?"

Noah scowled at him. "No, I didn't bag it."

"Damn."

"Did you learn anything?" Remy asked.

"Nothing new. I hung around Soma all night, but Bronwyn never showed."

Remy scowled. "What are you doing here, then?"

Gregor lifted an eyebrow. "It's near dawn. I had to get out of the light. It wouldn't do to be caught at the Orchid all day. A man can only take so much pop music." He looked around at them. "You all should get some rest, as well. You all look like hell."

Skye sighed. "Greg's right. We should get some sleep. I need to make some calls tomorrow."

"I'll keep trying to track down the scientists," Fallon said.

"No." Skye glared at her. "Bed. Now."

She sighed, but she didn't argue as they all trudged upstairs to their rooms. They didn't all live at HQ. Fallon had a small townhouse in a fashionable neighborhood, and Gregor had a secret light-tight haunt somewhere he didn't talk about. They usually hung around when they were working a case, though. They spent so much time at work, it seemed pointless to live anywhere else.

As the first rays of sun blazed on the horizon, the Agency drifted into troubled sleep.

* * *

Light filtered through the gaps in the dark curtains covering Remy's bedroom windows. He didn't move for several seconds after waking. His body ached. A tight ball of tension coiled in his belly. His dark energy wanted out. He laid still. He took a deep breath and let it out in a long, slow breath. His throat burned as the pent up magic hissed out of his body.

He sighed in relief and sat up. The mornings were getting worse. The dark magic inside him was desperate for release. A human body could not contain it for long. It wanted out. He stretched laboriously, grimacing slightly against the pain. He rose and when he did, his body felt almost normal again. He still felt wound up, but he had a patchwork monster upon which he could unleash the pent up energy. It was his lucky day.

He checked his watch. It was only noon. He hadn't slept long. Since he'd touched the artifact five years ago, he hadn't slept much. He hadn't needed to. He stripped out of his clothes and stepped into the shower. He sighed contentedly as the hot spray of water pelted his skin and soothed the aching muscles.

His skin felt oddly hot. It wasn't an effect of his dark energy. Bad juju hung in the air. Not his bad juju. It felt alien and ominous. Something bad was coming. It might already be here. Something was about to happen.

He didn't like this part of the investigation. He didn't like the wait and see stage before the big break that solved the case. He didn't like not knowing what course to follow. He didn't think Bronwyn Liddle was responsible for the patchwork monsters, but his instincts were resolved on one thing, and that was finding her. Even if she wasn't involved in the creature attacks or the disappearances, she was important.

He would find her if it was the last thing he did. It probably would be.

If she wasn't involved with his case, there was some other reason she was in town. She was hunting something. Perhaps she was on a personal vendetta. It wouldn't be the first time he crossed paths with vengeful vampires. Sometimes he stopped them. Other times, it was better to look the other way. Sometimes it was better to stake them all and sort it out later.

As he dressed, he wished it was night. He didn't see much of the daylight these days. Even when he was awake, he spent most of his time indoors doing research or talking to assets. He liked the night. It drew him. He wanted to patrol the streets and find and kill the patchwork monster before it hurt anyone else. He itched for action. It felt as though his skin was on wrong. Perhaps a good monster hunt and kill would sooth the jumping beans in his belly.

Fallon was not at her computer when Remy strode into the lab. Skye was. He did not turn around to greet him. He met Remy's eyes in the reflection of his glass monitor for a split second, then turned back to his screen.

"Anything new?"

Skye shook his head. "Not really. We've spoken to a few of the scientists on the list. A couple of them are dead. Three are unaccounted for. There are another three to talk to before we can make a suspect list."

"It sounds like a needle in a haystack."

"It's not as bad as all that. The list is short enough."

"We might have better luck canvassing the neighborhood, going door to door."

Skye considered this. "It might be a last resort. We could end up knocking on doors in the areas of the attacks, see if anything comes up."

"I do a love a good last resort."

"We have plenty of other dead ends to chase down first."

"Right." Remy sighed. He scrubbed a hand down his cheek as he peered up at the topographical map on the screen above Noah's console. The usual red and yellow blotches colored the clear glass. There wasn't any new paranormal activity. In fact, the hot spots were a little less hot these days. He wasn't sure how he'd missed it. Even the vamps and werewolves who hadn't been taken were leaving the city in droves. That wasn't normally considered a bad thing. Now, though, Remy felt a deep sense of foreboding.

Skye looked up at him. "It's been fluctuating for years. It's nothing to be concerned about."

"But there is. Someone is snatching them and doing horrible experiments on them."

Skye sighed. "Yes, I suppose you're right."

"Where's Fallon? I expected to find her here looking like a junkie just off their last fix."

"I made her go to bed hours ago. I'm not sure when she'll wake up."

"If she wakes up. I'm worried about her. She's been on the juice again."

"She needs it to keep her head from spiraling off. She's got a lot of power inside her building up and bursting out."

Remy glanced away.

Skye lifted a shrewd eyebrow. "She'll be okay."

"She won't. We need to do something about her."

"She can take care of herself."

"Really? You're just going to leave it like that?"

"Nothing I say is going to help. She will make her own decisions. I have tried to help her. She won't accept it. It just sends her further back down the spiral."

He spun in his chair to peer up at Remy. "I've seen her like this before, Rem. She pulls out of it."

"But for how long? This is going to kill her eventually."

"So are her powers."

Remy blinked. "What?"

"You think someone can hold that much energy inside forever? The human body can't contain it. She can't eat or drink enough to keep up with it."

Remy sighed. His stomach roiled uneasily. He wasn't the same as Fallon. He turned away.

Skye stared at him as though he knew exactly what he was thinking. "What are you going to do today?"

"I want to find Bronwyn Liddle. I think she holds the key to all of this."

Skye frowned. "Why? She doesn't appear to have anything to do with this."

"I need to know why she's here. Even if it isn't related, she might have some information."

Remy was surprised when Skye didn't argue. "You're going to have to wait until nightfall."

"I know." Remy sighed. "I suppose I could take the instruments and comb the Tenderloin for a few hours, see if I can notice any unusual resonances in the area. A lab full of vamps and weres should be registering off the scales, right?"

Skye considered this. He nodded. "Yes, I would think, unless our guy has some sort of special cloaking ability. He might, if he's familiar with our instruments."

"Sure, but that's no reason not to try."

"Naturally." He spun back to his computer screen. "Take Noah with you."

"I'm not sure he's up to it. We should give him a chance to recover."

"I performed the ritual perfectly. He's fine."

"I think he needs some time with Fallon."

Skye didn't not turn around. There was no expression in his voice. "Ah. Yes. Perhaps he can monitor the maps and help us chase down some leads on the scientists."

Remy snorted. "He'll just love that."

"Just take your things and go."

Remy smirked. He opened the equipment cabinet on the opposite side of the room. He selected the resonance monitor from the padded foam shelf. It looked like a smart phone with a long, slender antenna. He slid it into his back pocket.

Skye did not even need to turn around. "Do not put that there. Use the case. For god's sake. That's a very delicate and expensive instrument."

Remy rolled his eyes. He tucked the monitor into a duffel bag. He stepped over to the weapons case. He tossed a few polished metal stakes into the bag. And a large hunting knife. A 9mm pistol with silver bullets. What killed demons? Better to be safe than sorry. He grabbed the crossbow. And a vial of acid. Demons hated acid.

"Are you really expecting to run across a supernatural army?"

Remy paused. "From the look of Noah last night, yes."

He watched the buildings pass swiftly by as he steered the black Agency issue SUV through the streets of Outer Sunset toward the Tenderloin. He liked San Francisco, but it wasn't home. He liked the Bay and the Golden Gate bridge. He liked the quaint neighborhoods and the pulsating nightlife. He liked the feeling of life and vitality that ran through every neighborhood, even the darker, seedier ones. They had even more life than the others. He even liked the fog. It seemed appropriate somehow.

But it wasn't home. He couldn't go home. He could never go home again.

It was still early in the day. The sun was shining, but it the air was dense and chilly. It was usually chilly. He didn't mind. He swung the SUV abruptly into a small space in front of the Black Java coffee shop. It was a tiny, hole in the wall place with concrete walls hung with local art available for purchase at exorbitant prices. A few of the spaces were empty, as though someone had recently purchased the pieces and the owners hadn't replaced them yet.

Black Java smelled strongly of herbal tea. Remy wasn't interested in tea. When he strode to the textured stone counter, the girl behind the register flashed him a wide, bright smile. She wore a long, blonde ponytail. She looked young and fresh. She was chatty. "Hi there. Welcome to Black Java. How are you today?"

He lifted a single eyebrow. He wasn't interested in small talk. "Fine, thanks."

"What are you up to today? Are you on your lunch hour?"

He smirked slightly. Lunch hour. He didn't think he'd ever had a lunch hour in his life. "Nah. I'm just getting started."

"Oh? What do you do?"

He resisted the urge to roll his eyes. People asked him this a lot. Why was it any of their business? "I'm in private investigations."

Her dark eyes widened. "Oh, that sounds exciting."

"It is. For instance, do you know any place where a guy might be splicing together creatures and turning them into new creatures?"

She grinned. "I love that cartoon."

"I hate it." He frowned at her in disappointment.

The barista looked a little put off. Her smile wavered, and she looked a little confused. "Ah, what can I get you?"

"Coffee. Black."

She nodded and turned away from him to fill a paper cup. When she turned back to him, she smiled half-heartedly. He handed her a five dollar bill and spun away from the counter without a word. He probably should have been a little more polite to her. She'd seemed like a nice enough girl.

Remy supposed he just wasn't that nice of a guy.

No one in the Tenderloin gave him a second glance as he wandered aimlessly through the streets with the resonance monitor. It bleeped a few times, and he chased the source with a racing pulse. Nothing happened. The hot spots were nothing more than Agency-sanctioned vampire nests or the left over energies from dimensional rifts. He sighed. Nothing. There was no hidden lab where vamps, werewolves and demons languished in cells or on gurneys with each other's limbs attached.

An involuntary shiver ran down his spine. It sounded horrible.

Could it be underground? He supposed it was possible. His instruments should have been able to pick it up. It had a long enough range to penetrate the bowels of one of the old, dilapidated brick buildings in the less fashionable parts of the neighborhood. It should have even been able to detect resonances in the highest rise buildings in the city.

He glared at the instrument and beat it against him palm a few times. That had helped when he was a kid, but modern, sophisticated technology didn't respond to physical violence as well as he would have liked. He sighed and stared up at a crumbling brick building. It might once have been a grand, thriving apartment where the wealthy and fashionable had lived. Now it looked as though it would be better off in the crosshairs of a wrecking ball.

Whoever was building these hybrid monsters must have some sort of protection from the Agency. That wasn't good.

The resonance monitor bleeped excitedly. Remy jumped and peered down at it. He held the small, slim instrument away from him. He spun in a circle. The resonance was coming from an alley between the tenement buildings. He followed it.

He heard a rustling in the alley a few feet away. He froze.

A small, shaggy dog rifled through a pile of trash and debris beside the dumpster. Remy sighed in relief and stepped toward it. The monitor shrieked. He lifted his eyebrows. It wasn't an ordinary dog.

The mutt stiffened and stepped away from the debris through which it had been nosing. He stared at Remy for several moments. Tension hung in the air around the dog. He growled low in his throat. Remy rolled his eyes and touched the gun on his belt.

The dog whimpered plaintively. He yapped once. Then he spun around and raced the other way. Remy smirked.

A shadow passed in front of his eyes, so quickly he might have imagined it.

He jumped and looked around in surprise. The monitor did not bleep. He blinked and looked around again. There was no dog, no shadow. He frowned. He was not traditionally the sort of person who imagined things. He stepped deeper into the alley. There was no one there but him.

His phone chirped insistently. He sighed and yanked it out of his jacket picket. "Yeah?"

Noah's voice was grim. "I think you should come back to the office. Something's wrong with Fallon."

Remy sighed. "I'm on my way."

* * *

"What's wrong with her?" Noah demanded, glaring at Skye as though he might be at fault for whatever was happening to Fallon.

"We can't keep her here like this," Remy said, frowning down at her.

"She's in some kind of trance. I'm doing the best I can," Skye replied tersely. He stood over Fallon, monitoring her with some sort of short, slender wand. The blonde woman rocked back and forth in the center of the lobby floor, clutching her knees to her chest. She didn't seem aware of them at all. Her eyes were rolled back in her head to show the whites. Her breath was soft and shallow. "She isn't giving off any energy."

"She is channeling it. It's all inside." He looked at Noah grimly. "It's going to burst. She's probably in the throes of a vision." He scowled at Skye. "It's because of the juice. It feels like it numbs the pain, but it just messes with the natural ebb and flow of her energies and power."

"This is not the time for a lecture."

"What do we do?" Noah asked, bending down on one knee to stare into Fallon's sheet white face. He lifted a hand as though he meant to touch her. Remy caught his wrist and shook his head.

"Normally, we wait it out." Skye frowned down at the wand. It didn't seem to have a screen. Remy wondered how he was reading it. "But her vital signs are slowing down increasingly. She's barely breathing. Her heart beat is faint. We can't let her keep fading or she will die."

Remy crossed his arms over his chest. "We could try to shock her out of it."

"Shock her?" Noah didn't sound as though he thought this was a very good idea.

"With electricity. Or with a psychic shock."

Skye and Noah turned to him with identical incredulous expressions. "With one of your blasts?" Noah demanded.

Remy shrugged. "It's all I've got. You can't choose your power."

Skye rolled his eyes. "You can choose not to absorb the energy from a dark artifact."

"Meaning have no power at all."

"Can we focus, please?" Noah demanded. "Do we have to banter about everything all of the time?"

"Yes. Don't underestimate the investigative benefit of good banter."

"Noah?" Skye asked. "What do you say? Shock her out of it?"

Noah leaned forward and pressed his fingers against Fallon's throat. Her pulse was a faint thump. His touch stirred her. She jerked slightly, and her breath hitched. She released her knees and tipped backward as though she'd lost control of her muscles. Noah exclaimed softly in concern and caught her before her head hit the marble floor. He brushed her long, stringy blonde hair gently from her face. He looked up. "Do it, Remy."

The corners of Remy's mouth twitched. "You'd better step away from her."

Skye took a hasty step back, but Noah hesitated. He didn't try to resist Remy's suggestion; he'd seen his dark energy blasts in action. He was strong but not that strong. He laid Fallon gently down on her back on the marble floor and stepped away from her to stand anxiously beside Skye.

"Gregor is going to be disappointed he missed this," Skye remarked.

Remy shrugged off his black leather jacket and let it fall to the floor. He rubbed his hands together. Already, wisps of black energy flowed from his fingertips. "Okay, I'm going to try to keep it small. Just a tiny little jolt."

Skye frowned skeptically. "Do you think you can?"

"Sure. The bursts I use in the field are usually big for a reason. I think I can localize it."

Skye took another step back.

Remy extended his hands and opened his palms toward the ceiling. The wisps of energy engulfed his hands so they were lost in the swirl of darkness. He felt a surge of strength. Power coursed through his body. He felt taut and alive. He felt good for the first time in days. He felt the energy trying to burst out of him in an intense, powerful pulse. He took a deep breath.

He could control the energy. It didn't control him. Not yet, anyway.

His gut tightened. He concentrated. The energy moved through his body. He clenched his teeth against the rush of built up power threatening to explode out of his fingertips. He exhaled slowly. A tiny, gentle stream of the pulsating darkness inside him surged from his fingers.

Fallon's entire body jerked in a long, slow convulsion. Then she was still.

Noah rushed forward, but Remy threw out an arm to stop him. "What happened?" Noah growled. "Did you hurt her? Is she alive?"

Skye knelt beside Fallon and checked her vitals. He glanced up at them with a grim expression. "She's alive. Actually, her signs are better."

Fallon suddenly shot up and gasped. Skye reared away from her and landed gracelessly on his backside. Remy lifted an eyebrow. He lowered his arm. Noah skidded to the ground beside Fallon, but he didn't touch her.

"Noah, get back," Remy barked. "She's having a vision. Don't touch her."

Noah flailed his arms around her, but he didn't touch her. She groaned and leaned forward between her knees, clutching her head. "I see her." Her voice was a low, raspy wail. "Bronwyn. I see her. Body parts. She's surrounded by body parts. There's blood everywhere. It looks like a slaughter house. Body parts everywhere. It's horrible!"

"What's she doing?" Remy demanded, dropping to a knee beside her.

"She has a knife."

"What's she doing with it?" Noah asked. "Is she the killer?"

Fallon moaned in an agonized crescendo. "There's someone with her. A man. A human man."

"What's she doing?"

"She stabbed him! She killed him. There's more. There's something else. Someone else around her—nearby—" She lifted her head. Her eyes flew open, and she blinked around at them with a grimace. "No. That's it. It's all I can see. I'm sorry."

"It's okay," Noah said earnestly. "It's okay, Fallon. You did a lot. You helped." He clutched her shoulders and lifted her carefully to her feet. She wobbled. He hoisted her arm around her shoulder and wrapped his arm around her waist. He glanced at Remy and Skye. "I'm going to take her upstairs. She needs to rest."

Remy nodded. "Okay. Thanks, Fallon. Take care of her, Noah."

Skye watched after Fallon and Noah until they'd disappeared up the staircase and into the hallway leading to the bedrooms. He glanced at Remy. "Okay. So maybe you're right. Maybe Bronwyn Liddle has something to do with the monster maker."

Remy lifted his chin. "I'll track her down."

Skye nodded. "When night falls, take the team and pick her up in Soma."

* * *

"The stubborn prick," Noah complained. He glared across the Bleeding Orchid toward the cloud of acrid, grey smoke that surrounded Merek.

The old vampire didn't meet Noah's glower. He lifted his chin and avoided looking at the table where Noah sat with Remy and Gregor. There was no expression on his face, but the corners of Merek's mouth were tight with irritation. He wanted nothing to do with the Agency. If he'd had a choice, he would have had them instantly ousted from the premises.

Luckily there wasn't a damn thing he could do about them. They were the law around there.

"Do you think she's going to show up?" Noah asked, frowning.

"I don't know. It depends." Gregor leaned back in his chair and smiled around at the two young girls hovering on the edges of their table as though they were waiting for an invitation to approach. They wore short, black dresses and too much makeup. He looked at Remy as if for permission to call them to him.

Remy scowled at him and shot the girls such a dark glare, they skittered away. He looked back at his partners as though nothing had happened. Gregor puffed out his thick bottom lip in a pout.

"Do you think Merek warned her?" Noah stared at the vampire as though he could light him on fire with his mind. Merek had refused to call Bronwyn to set up a meeting, but that didn't mean he didn't know how to reach her.

"Yes. I'm fairly sure he did that," Remy replied. "At least we'll find out if she's interested in playing with us or not."

After a few more hours of the same, they had to admit she probably wasn't. Gregor had tried to hold out for as long as he could, but about an hour into the stake out, he'd disappeared into a dark corner with the two goth girls. He hadn't returned. Remy hoped there was something left of them when Gregor was through paying them his attention.

Noah sighed. Merek hadn't moved. They'd been watching vampires and their dates writhing all over each other for about long enough. "She's not coming. He must have warned her."

Remy nodded his agreement. "We'd better find Greg. He's probably neck deep in some underage juvenile delinquent by now."

"Man, I hate this place so much."

"It isn't so bad. At least the view is nice."

"If you like vamps or vamp groupies, which I do not."

Remy snorted. "Come on. We've got better things to do than stake out a vamp bar."

"Yeah. I want a re-match with that patchwork monster. It's still early enough to patrol."

Remy rose. "We can come back tomorrow night and try again. She has to show up eventually. I'll find Gregor." His eyes darted anxiously back and forth as he stalked the perimeter of the bar. His nerves sang. He didn't want to leave. She was coming. If it took days, he intended to be there when she arrived. Just now, though, he didn't have the luxury of days. There were bigger problems in the city, and he was responsible for solving them.

He hadn't been wrong about Gregor. The swarthy vamp was ensconced in a corner with the two goth girls. The blonde girl perched on his lap, her mouth lolling as he sucked from the puncture wound in her neck. He absently kneaded her exposed breast. The darker girl looked as though he'd already taken his fill of her blood. She slouched beside him with her hand down the waistband of his pants. She stroked him languidly up and down. Gregor's free hand moved under her skirt. Her head fell back. She groaned almost lazily.

Remy rolled his eyes. "All right, that's enough."

Gregor snapped to attention immediately. He withdrew from the girls. They didn't move. They remained on the dark velvet cushions as though they were too drunk or weak to stand. They mewled in disappointment and clutched at him. He batted their hands gently away. "You find her?" he asked, straightening his clothes shamelessly. His erection strained against the front of his skin tight black pants.

"Nah. It doesn't look like she's coming. Come on. Go wash your hands and—whatever and let's get out on the streets. We should patrol before dawn."

Gregor sighed, but he didn't argue. He was only gone for a few seconds. He looked as though he'd had several moments to clean himself up. He nodded. "I'm ready."

Noah scowled at them as they approached, but he didn't say anything. He wasn't as cavalier as Remy when it came to Gregor's bloodlust. He didn't like being reminded that his partner was a lascivious vampire who required blood and sex to survive. Perhaps he didn't need the sex quite as much, but he seemed to enjoy it, right enough.

There was no noise in the alley outside the Bleeding Orchid. There weren't any vagrants or couples sneaking an intimate moment around the back of the building. There weren't even any rats. The air crackled with tension.

Gregor crouched suddenly. He tilted his head as though he was listening to something in the distance. There was no expression on his face, but his eyes darted cagily around them. Remy felt whatever it was he was hearing. The air seemed charged. His nerves jangled, and he stiffened in attention. Energy roiled in his gut as though it meant to burst out in a shield to protect him from whatever approached. Noah recognized his partners' reactions. His shackles rose. He touched the gun on his holster.

They spun as one toward the back of the alley, where the darkness enveloped the trash and debris beyond the club. Mist swirled up from the ground as though a fog was rolling in.

And then she was there. She might have materialized out of the mist or moved so quickly, even Gregor hadn't seen her. Her long, black coat billowed out behind her as though she'd stepped into a breeze. They couldn't see her face in the darkness, but she carried a long, thin blade like a short sword or long dagger. It extended from the silhouette of her arm as though it were part of her. Her dark red hair glinted like blood in the faint, flickering lights above their heads.

Her voice was a quiet, husky murmur. It carried with eerie clarity through the electric silence. A strange sensation crept along Remy's spine. Inside him, his dark magic was like a cyclone ravaging his body.

"I hear you're looking for me. I'm Bronwyn Liddle."

She strode toward them. She moved so quickly, Gregor reacted almost involuntarily. His fangs protracted, and he hissed like a cat. Remy didn't move; he was waiting to see what she'd do. Noah raised a crossbow to his shoulder.

Seconds later, Bronwyn Liddle was holding his weapon. Noah started belatedly and cursed.

And then the woman rose abruptly, effortlessly up into the air to hover several feet above them. She seemed almost to be floating. They could see her face now in the flickering light. Her large dark, almond shaped eyes glittered angrily, and she hissed back at them through her long, sharp white fangs. For a moment, they stared up at her in shock. Then they crouched, preparing for her attack.

"I don't want to hurt you." Her voice was almost gentle, despite the animal rage on her beautiful, ivory pale face. Her long hair swirled around her like a blood-soaked storm cloud. She seemed to be shimmering in the faint streetlight, as though a halo of energy surrounded her entire body.

"Don't worry," Noah replied. He drew a large, long-barreled gun from the holster on his hip and aimed it at her. "You won't."

"Fine." Her fangs gleamed as if they were lit from within.

She spun abruptly in mid-air. Then she plummeted toward them.

From inside Remy, the pent up energy exploded involuntarily outward in an intense pulse of deadly, consuming darkness. His entire body racked as though electricity coursed through him. Bronwyn Liddle dropped unceremoniously like a bird shot dead out of the air. Remy rushed forward to catch her before she hit the ground. He staggered slightly under her weight and dropped to his knees.

He brushed the tangled, wavy red hair from her face. She didn't look like a killer or a demon now. She looked peaceful. She almost looked sweet. She was very beautiful. They were all very beautiful. And they all looked harmless as they slept. He glanced up at his partners. "She'll be out a couple minutes, at least. We can get her to HQ without a fight."

"Wow, man," Noah muttered, staring down at the unconscious vampire. "She really can fly."

"And I think she would have killed us," Gregor added. He held himself a few steps away from Remy and the woman. He didn't seem to watch to touch her. Remy didn't really blame him. She felt strange in his arms. She was as soft as silk and as deadly as a viper. A strange sort of tremor ran through her body, as though it could barely contain the power inside. It felt oddly familiar.

He stared down at her. Her full, ruby red lips parted slightly with her breath. Her dark lashes fell in half moons across her flawless, porcelain pale cheeks. She looked like a doll. She looked as though she might break in his arms if he handled her carelessly. She wouldn't, and if she awoke, she could rip his throat out before he even knew she'd moved. He shook his head.

"I'm not so sure about that. I think she thought she was acting in self-defense."

"I think that bad juju is affecting your brain," Noah told him sharply.

Gregor smirked. "That or the hot vamp chick."

Remy glared at him. "Let's get out of here. We got what we came for. I want to get off the streets before someone sees us and decides to fight us for her."

"Or she wakes up," Noah said grimly. "That would be even worse."

CHAPTER FOUR

Bronwyn awoke abruptly. She was on her feet before she'd fully opened her eyes. She was in a small metal cell. She lifted her eyebrows. It hummed. The bars in front of her looked strangely liquid, as though made of some alien metal. She stepped forward and touched them. They thrummed under her fingers, as if they were magically charged.

She chuckled low in her throat. She knew exactly where she was. The Agency.

The room beyond her cell was small and featureless. There was a table with two chairs and an empty jug of water. She felt the static magical purr of the cells around her. There were more. She paused and listened. They were all empty. She was the only captive in this prison.

She paced the small space for a few moments. She touched the walls. They hummed with the same electricity. Interesting. She'd heard of these cells. The charges were meant to inhibit psychic abilities. Quash magical resonances. She smirked. When she wished to leave, she would. Their tricks would do little to stop her.

Just now, though, she was right where she wanted to be. She sat down on the floor and crossed her legs. It wouldn't hurt to wait it out. This Agency duty station seemed slightly more interesting than the others. She'd been hearing things about the team all over the community. She'd come all this way. She might as well meet the opposition.

She didn't have to wait long. She heard three people descend the stairs to the left of her cell. She did not rise to meet them. She sensed the vampire and the soldier she'd met in the alley. She didn't recognize the other. The chaotic swirl of psychic energy did not feel the same as Remy St. John's dark, heady power. Ah. It must be the woman. Fallon Weir.

She smiled as they approached her. She knew them all. "Ah. And here they are. I was wondering when you would come."

The vampire and the soldier watched her with identical alert, wary gazes. Fallon glared at her through glittering, translucent eyes. She didn't look afraid. Her lip curled in loathing. Bronwyn studied her for the briefest moment, as though she might read the thoughts that were causing such open hostility. Bronwyn lifted an eyebrow.

"So," she said conversationally. "Would you care to explain to me why you attacked and arrested an innocent woman in a dark alley?"

"I hardly think you're innocent," Noah growled.

She considered this. "That's true. I'm not sure innocent is the correct terminology." She smiled at them. It was a gleaming, fangy smile. "Do you always treat people this way when you want to ask them something?"

"You're not a person." Fallon glared at her.

Bronwyn's eyes flicked to the vampire for a split second. He looked slightly offended, but he lifted his strong, smooth chin. "Ah. I see. I understand. So, if I were still a fragile, powerless human, you might be more polite."

"If you were human, you wouldn't need to be in this cage," Fallon replied coldly.

"That's pretty narrow-minded, considering who is standing beside you, psychic."

Fallon's pale skin colored slightly. Gregor didn't look at her. His jaw tightened. "What are you doing in San Francisco?" he asked in a civil voice.

She lifted her eyebrows. "I don't believe that has anything to do with the Agency."

"Let us be the judge of that."

She smiled. "I don't have to. I've done nothing. You attacked me, and now you are holding me against my will without charges."

"We have the right to detain hostiles when they present a danger to us," Noah told her.

"Now, who is hostile? It was you who attacked me in that alley. I said I didn't want to fight. I didn't try to hurt anyone."

Fallon didn't look convinced. Her lips pursed. Gregor glanced at Noah uncomfortably. Fallon might have sensed their unease. "She's a murderer," she reminded them sharply. "We all know about you, Bronwyn Liddle."

"Do you?"

"People die all around you."

Bronwyn considered this. Her mouth turned up slightly at the corners. "That is an oversimplification."

"I saw you kill a man! A human man."

98

She lifted an eyebrow. "When? In your head?" She stepped forward. She met Fallon's eyes. Her voice was low, husky and hypnotic. "Is that all you saw? You saw more than that, didn't you?"

Gregor and Noah turned to look at Fallon. The color drained from her face, but she did not meet their gazes. She lifted her chin. Her lip curled. "She isn't going to talk. She has information we need. I saw it. She knows what's going on."

"I think we should wait for Remy--" Noah began, frowning nervously.

"He's still out from the blast. Who knows how long he'll be. People are dying!" Fallon glared at Bronwyn. "Tell us what you know about the scientist."

Bronwyn blinked in surprise. "What scientist?"

"The one who is making monsters!"

She didn't know about any scientists. "Tell me about him."

"Don't pretend you aren't involved."

"Involved?"

"Did you see something, Fallon?" Noah asked. "What did you see?"

Gregor shook his head slowly from side to side. "I don't think she's involved with the scientist."

"Some crack team you are." Bronwyn smirked. "Do you think you should talk amongst yourselves and get your suspicions straight?"

"Noah, use the gun."

The men looked at her in naked shock. "What?"

"We need to know how to stop the scientist!"

"I don't know about any scientist."

"You're lying! I saw you! Noah, use the gun!"

Gregor took a step forward to face him. "Noah, I don't think--"

Noah stared at Fallon. Her translucent eyes were wide and wild. They practically burned. He hoisted a wide, long-barreled weapon onto his shoulder. It looked like a cannon, but the end of the barrel wasn't an opening; it was a strange, thick glass lid. It glinted slightly blue in the bright florescent light overhead. Bronwyn eyed it in interest, but Gregor reared back as though Noah had already fired at him.

"Noah!"

Bronwyn rolled her eyes and pointed a finger at her chest. "I am a vampire, you know. Guns don't actually hurt me, no matter how large they are."

"This one will." Fallon's voice was low and cold. "Noah!"

He did not argue with her. Gregor dove for cover and cowered behind the table. A short, radiant blast of purple light struck Bronwyn full in the face. "Noah, no!" Gregor shouted.

Bronwyn blinked at them. She crossed her arms over her chest with a bored expression. "What was that?"

They stared at her for several long, silent moments. Gregor lifted his head. He looked shocked. "It's UV."

Bronwyn rolled her eyes. "You know, if that had worked on me that would have been a very nasty thing to do."

"It didn't work," Noah muttered bemusedly.

"Have you been studying vampire hunting according to Blade comics? What sort of place do you run here? Do you always torture innocent paranormals when they don't answer your questions the way you want them to?" She didn't sound angry. She sounded disappointed.

The door slammed against the wall as Remy stormed into the room. He looked between them with an austere expression. When he spotted the UV cannon, he scowled at his team. "What the hell is going on in here?"

Bronwyn turned her dark, electric eyes on him. She lifted an eyebrow. "She isn't affected by sunlight," Gregor told him as though this explained everything.

Remy's shoulders stiffened. His brilliant blue eyes glinted angrily. "You used the gun on her? Did she attack?"

"I didn't attack. I stood here and attempted to be cooperative. Your team here didn't like my responses."

Gregor stalked slowly toward the bars as if to study an interesting but very dangerous specimen. "How come the gun didn't hurt you?"

Bronwyn lifted her chin. "Sunlight hasn't hurt me for fifty years."

His mouth dropped open. He didn't seem to know what to say. "Is that how it works?"

"Not for you it won't."

Noah looked uncomfortable, but Fallon's eyes still glittered with wild, furious hatred. "She's involved in all this, and she refuses to talk."

"No. I refuse to say what you want me to say."

"You're involved in this!"

"Saying it over and over with increasing emphasis is not going to make it any truer. I'm not involved with any scientists, but if you ask the right questions, you might learn something that could help you." Bronwyn's eyes met Remy's. He was like a radiant light in darkness. He was in brilliant color. The others were in drab, colorless grey. "It seems as if you all have a lot to learn."

Remy strode forward to face her directly. For a moment, he said nothing. He held her gaze as though he was attempting to unravel a complicated riddle. There was no emotion in his expression, but his blue eyes flashed and smoldered as if there was flame inside him. Bronwyn lifted her chin and regarded him with equal heat.

"Do you know about the scientist making creatures?" His voice was low and even.

She lifted a shoulder in a delicate shrug. "I don't know about any scientist." She jerked her chin toward the team. "Send your flunkies out and we can talk about what I do know."

Noah squared his shoulders and frowned. "We're not going anywhere. We interrogate prisoners together."

Remy half turned his head, though his eyes never left Bronwyn. He lifted a hand. "Go."

Noah scowled. Bronwyn sensed he was bridling under the command. He looked as if he intended to argue or remind Remy he wasn't in charge of this team, no matter how often they looked to him for leadership.

"I can handle this. You've done enough." There was no inflection in his voice, but the reaction was intense. They all colored in unease. "This is not generally how we work."

"You mean acting on a jealous junkie's rage?" Her voice was soft. Only Remy and Gregor heard it. "I hadn't really expected a great level of professionalism from the Agency, so you needn't concern yourself with my impressions."

Now Remy turned his head to look at his team. His brow furrowed as he stared long and hard at Fallon. She dipped her head to avoid his scrutiny. "All of you. Go."

They didn't need to be told a third time. They turned and filed out of the room.

Bronwyn smiled through her gleaming fangs. "Ah. They don't like that, do they? Taking orders from the Pure Power. But you aren't *Castus Vox* anymore, are you?"

He frowned at her. He did not reply to this.

Her smile wasn't malicious. "Ah, yes. I know all about you, Remy St. John. I know all about all of you. You're only here as punishment. How do the others feel about being second string to someone who's only here because he's forced to be?"

"You know nothing about me and my team."

"You're wrong about that. You think you can come looking for me without my finding out? You think I didn't ask about you all? I know all about you." She lifted an eyebrow. "Do you think you would have found me if I hadn't wanted you to? I went to you. You attacked me."

He considered this. She was speaking the truth. He seemed to realize this, but he didn't move toward her. "Are you trying to get me to let you out of the cage?"

She laughed. "If I wanted out of the cage, I would be out of the cage."

Remy looked as though he believed her. "You wanted to get in here?"

"I go anywhere I like. I wanted to meet the people who were hunting me. It sounds like you have quite a situation on your hands. You want to talk about it?"

He scowled. "You expect me to believe you aren't involved in all of this?"

"I assure you, I am involved. But not in the way you think."

"Are you trying to say you're on our side?"

"No. I'm definitely not on your side. I'm on my side."

"You're a vigilante."

"I am a hunter."

"You kill people."

"No. I kill murderers." He lifted an eyebrow. "And you—aren't you a little ball of black magic." When he scowled, she smiled at him. "That was quite a jolt you gave me." She moved so quickly, she was pressed against the charged, thrumming bars before he ever saw her move. She could have reached out and touched him if she wanted to. She could have seized his throat and yanked him forward, toward her razor sharp fangs.

He didn't step back. She could practically feel him vibrating. Energy pulsed around him. She reached out and ran a long, slender finger down his chest. His muscles contracted where she touched him. He exhaled sharply. He didn't move.

"All that black juju is just coming out of every pore in your body."

He scowled. "You don't know anything about me."

"You'll lose it, you know. You can't hold it all inside your body forever. It will seep out or it will consume you from the inside out. Just like your psychic friend. You know that, don't you? She's dying. All that power is just killing her."

He stared at her as though he could not look away. His voice was low and deep. "What are you trying to do?"

"I'm not trying to do anything. You're the one who brought me here. It's your party. Did you want to do the talking? This doesn't have to be complicated. You ask me what you want to know, and I will answer you truthfully."

"How can I trust you're telling the truth? Everywhere you go, death follows."

"You know all about me, don't you? Who told you? Was it the Agency? Or was it *Castus Vox*?"

He lifted an eyebrow. He actually looked curious. "What do you know about them?"

"I know all about them. I know they aren't just an order of white mages with the same goals as the Paranormal Sector of the Secret Service. I know they have power and ambition beyond their ostensibly benign goals. They're not just trying to keep evil from the hands of the innocents. They're much more sinister than all that. They have secrets you couldn't begin to imagine."

"You don't know what you're talking about."

"No? I've been around much longer than you. I've known them longer. I know many things you do not. You were never in the inner circle, though you might have been. You had a very promising career until you were tossed out on your ear for using that dark artifact." She smiled. "Tell me why you did it. You knew what would happen."

He gave the same rote answer he'd given for the last five years. "Its lure was irresistible. It's the nature of the artifact."

She laughed. Her fangs flashed. "And you wanted the power."

His mouth turned up slightly at the corners. His brilliant eyes glittered a little. "And I wanted the power."

"Now we're getting somewhere. You told me something true. Now I'll tell you something true. Go on. Now's your chance."

He considered her for a long moment. "Tell me about how you killed a dozen *Castus Vox*."

Bronwyn smiled. "Is that what your archive says?"

"No. Not exactly."

She thought about this and moved away from him to lean on the wall behind her. She regarded him. "I was there, but it wasn't what you're thinking. I was tracking a psychic killer across Ireland."

"A human?"

"Yes."

"You hunt humans."

"I hunt killers, human or otherwise."

He scowled. "That isn't for you to do."

"Who is to say? The Agency? *Castus Vox*? I've been around longer. If anyone should decide what's best for the world, it should be the ones who've been in it longer and will be in it long after they've died."

He paused. He looked as if he wasn't sure whether or not this was true. He didn't argue. "Go on."

"He used his empathy to kill his victims. Scare them or pleasure them to death. He begged asylum from the *Castus Vox* claiming a vampire was hunting him."

"One was."

"Yes. I was. And they should not have shielded him. I gave them a chance. I told them what he was and what he would do to them. I told them I would come in after him and there was nothing they could do to stop me."

"You killed them to get to him?"

She laughed for several seconds. "No. No, I didn't touch a single one. They were already dead when I got inside. He killed quickly. I was too late to save any of them." She lifted an eyebrow. "They didn't mention that in the file, did they?"

He stared at her. "No. They didn't mention that."

"There is a lot the *Castus Vox* leaves out of their reports."

"All right. So what are you doing in San Francisco?"

She smiled. "Taking a holiday. Everyone needs a mini-break now and again."

He frowned. "I don't believe that."

"I don't blame you. It's a lie. But you owe me an answer now."

"I didn't agree to that."

"You don't think it's fair? I am playing by your rules. I haven't even shown you how I could escape if I wanted."

He smirked. "I am actually very interested to know."

"I bet you are."

"Can you shape shift?"

She shrugged.

"The bars are charged with a magic inhibitor."

She laughed. "Yes, I had sussed that. They won't do much good. I can shape shift, but only in limited forms. I hate to do it." She lifted an eyebrow. "It ruins what I'm wearing, and wouldn't you agree this is a fantastic outfit?"

He smiled as she spun in a slow circle as if to display the long, black coat and tight, low slung black pants she wore. She tossed her head and squared her shoulders to display the ample cleavage above her black tank top to its greatest advantage. His eyes lingered on her smooth, ivory pale skin a moment. "It's very nice."

"Please. You've been thinking about how to tear it off me since you walked in the door."

He laughed. "All right. You can have your question."

"What scientist were they talking about?"

He thought about this for a moment. "We're investigating attacks by a creature which appears to be part vampire, two parts werewolf and unknown parts demon."

"Tooth, claw and venom." She frowned. "That's troubling."

"There have been a large number of vampire and werewolf disappearances in the last couple months."

She nodded. "Yes. I'm here investigating the disappearances. A friend of mine, Linus Gunderson, was taken in Chicago. I have been tracking his scent across the country, but I keep losing him. I learned about the new disappearances from Merek. I didn't know about the wolves." She stepped forward to face him. There was no mischief or playfulness in her expression now. "So some scientist is combining them together to create...what? Ultimate monsters?"

"Apparently."

"That's horrifying."

"Yes. It is."

"You could have just gotten to that in the beginning. It might have saved us all a lot of trouble."

"But it would not have been near as much fun."

She lifted an eyebrow. "Ah. Did you enjoy our game, Agent St. John?"

"Remy."

"All right."

"It was informative."

"Indeed it was. Are we finished?"

He peered at her for several seconds. His electric eyes glittered. "I think we could come to some arrangement."

"Arrangement?"

"We could work together."

She laughed. "Work together. Right. Why not?"

"I'm guessing you lost Linus' trail again." Her silence confirmed his guess. "Maybe when he was spliced with something else, you lost his scent."

Her expression was suddenly grim. "Yes. I lost him."

"So we're searching for the same place. The scientist's lab."

She frowned. "Your psychic said she saw me kill someone. Perhaps it was the scientist."

"I don't condone the murder of humans."

106

"You're the one who wanted to work with me. You'll have to accept my methods."

He narrowed his eyes. "We can save this argument for a more opportune moment."

"Sure. I'm willing to accept we might need to work together to solve your case and retrieve my friend."

"How good of a friend are we talking?"

She smirked. "Just a friend. Nothing more. So. I will allow you to let me out of the cage now."

"Allow me?" He lifted his eyebrows.

"I told you I can get out whenever I wish."

"I would like to see that."

"Don't be so confident. These inhibitors won't work on me."

"It's win-win for me. Either they don't, or that fantastic outfit is ruined."

She moved so fast, he didn't see how she'd done it. She was beside him in the blink of an eye. She pressed against him. He could feel the firm softness of her breasts against his shoulder. He didn't move. Her voice was a husky, sensual murmur in his ear. "Is that what you want? To see me naked? That's not very professional." Her tongue darted out to swirl along the shell of his ear. He shivered slightly. Heat pulsed from his rigid body. She stepped away from him. He spun to face her and looked down at her body with hot, glittering eyes. She was dressed. He sighed in disappointment. She laughed. "Are we done here?"

"Yeah. We're done. Come on. I need to explain this to the others."

"I'm sure it's going to go over very, very well."

* * *

Noah and Gregor shot to their feet in a single, fluid motion when Remy and Bronwyn strode side by side into the lobby. Noah stepped in front of Fallon as if to shield her from the escapee.

"She's out of the cage!" Noah said. "Why is she out of the cage?"

Bronwyn smirked. She was beside him before anyone saw her move. He jumped at her sudden proximity. Fallon reared backward and ducked behind Gregor. "What's the matter, soldier?" Bronwyn purred. "Afraid I'll take revenge on you for attempting to kill me with artificial sunlight?"

Remy stiffened and took a step forward, but Bronwyn didn't touch Noah. Noah shivered all the same. "Is she allowed to do that?" Gregor demanded. "She shouldn't be allowed to do that. I'm not allowed to do that. I have to walk around like a regular person."

"New rule," Remy said. He scowled. "No more doing that."

"Are you talking about the moving quickly or making your team... uncomfortable?' She snapped her teeth at Noah. He leaned away from her.

"Let's make it both," Noah put in. "How about that?"

Skye strode into the lobby with his head in a book. He looked up at them all in surprise. He blinked several times behind his rimless glasses, as though he wasn't sure what he was seeing. Bronwyn stepped away from Noah to stand beside Remy. As soon as she did, his shoulders relaxed. "Who is this?" Skye demanded.

"Skye Blayne, this is Bronwyn Liddle," Remy told him.

She smiled toothily at Skye. "Oh." Skye nodded. "I see. You found her."

"Yes."

"I expected her to be in a holding cell."

"I was. You team is very keen." Bronwyn told him wryly.

He lifted his eyebrows. "Yes. They are keen. So, I assume she's innocent, then?"

"No," Noah growled. "Not innocent."

"We're hunting the same creature," Remy added.

"All right. I assume we have sorted out our differences, then? We're working together?" Skye looked at Bronwyn.

She inclined her head. "I've been tracking a friend of mine across the country. He was taken in Chicago."

"Chicago? I didn't realize our guys had gotten that far north." Skye frowned. "I will research that right away. Maybe the duty station there can tell us more."

"I lost his scent there. He was always steps ahead. I found where he'd been but never where he was. I was able to pick up his scent again as he crossed the country, and each time it was the same. When I found where he'd been kept, he was already gone. I followed him here, and now his scent is completely gone."

"It might be masked somehow," Gregor mused. "It might not mean he's already been spliced."

"He he," Noah muttered. "Spliced."

Bronwyn glanced at Noah, then back at Remy. "Is he retarded?"

"It's a stupid cartoon."

"Cartoon?"

"You haven't seen it?" Noah asked.

She looked at him as though he were a small, idiotic child. "I don't watch cartoons. So how do we proceed?"

"How do you normally proceed?" Skye sounded genuinely interested.

She sighed. "I ask around, sniff out my prey. I'm a vamp. How else would I find my quarry? I don't have all your sophisticated equipment. I don't need it."

"It wouldn't matter if you did have it," Remy told her grimly. "We haven't gotten anywhere with it."

"So that's why you're hunting me down? You had no better lead?"

They all glanced around at each other. "That is a little true," Gregor admitted.

She rolled her eyes. "Okay, so now what? I haven't gotten any leads, either. No one seems to know anything more than that my people are disappearing. They don't even know as much as you lot, for once."

"You'd better come into the lab." Skye tilted his head at her. He didn't seem to have any problem thinking of her as an ally rather than an enemy. The others, though, held back as though she might suddenly lunge at them with her fangs bared.

She seemed to enjoy their discomfort. Remy rolled his eyes and followed her and Skye into the lab. Skye sat down in front of his console and punched up the topographical map. Bronwyn stepped toward the huge glass monitor with interest. "Very sophisticated," she remarked. "I did not expect that."

"The government has very cool toys," Skye said. He pointed toward the five red dots sprinkled on the map. "These are the areas of the creature attacks."

Fallon slipped past Bronwyn to sit down in front of her screen. Her shoulders were rigid. Bronwyn stepped closer to Remy with the tiniest smirk on her lips. Remy inhaled deeply. Her scent was heady and intoxicating, like roses and some sort of musk that was uniquely hers. He didn't step away from her. Almost unconsciously, he moved closer so her scent filled his senses.

Noah leaned over Fallon's shoulder to point at the screen. Fallon did not even seem to notice him. Her ears were pink, and her jaw was tight. "So the attacks are happening in a localized place," she added tightly. "We think the creature—"

"Or creatures," Skye put in grimly.

"—has escaped the lab at these times to hunt."

"We think it's been captured again each time," Noah added. "We suspect it's otherwise contained."

"What is this area?" Bronwyn asked.

"The Tenderloin."

"Okay. I'd like to sniff out the neighborhood, see if I can discover anything that might be helpful."

"It probably won't do much good," Remy said darkly. "Our equipment hasn't picked anything up."

"I'm not using any equipment." She turned her head to meet his gaze. "I'm using my senses. They're better than any of your equipment could ever hope to be."

He shrugged. "It's worth a shot. Nothing else has turned anything up."

"I'm still working the scientists." Fallon's voice was slightly sharp, as if Bronwyn's disdain for their equipment had been a deep insult. "I think we might have narrowed it down to Dr. Ambrose Fisk, a biochemist from D.C. He worked for the Agency for several years in their research lab there."

Bronwyn's expression tightened. "I know about the research labs. They keep paranormals there in large glass rooms, trying to figure out what makes us tick."

"Yeah, well, he got a little keen," Skye put in, squinting at Fallon's screen. "He was forced to resign about five years ago."

"He's in San Francisco?" Remy lifted his eyebrows.

"No," Fallon replied. "We just haven't tracked him down yet. The rest of the scientists on the list have been cleared."

"Okay. This is good," Noah said, as though someone were finally speaking some sense. "It's a lead."

"We're searching property records for anything rented or owned by Dr. Fisk. It might turn something up." She shrugged. "It might not. It's worth a shot, anyway."

Remy looked at Bronwyn. "I'll take you to the Tenderloin."

She smirked and glanced around at the others. "Anyone else care to join us?"

Gregor opened his mouth to reply, but Remy shot him a piercing look. Gregor sighed. "Noah and I can patrol the neighborhood in case the creature escapes and attacks again."

"It's nearly dawn," Skye warned.

"Fine," Bronwyn said. "I can work in the daytime."

"I beg your pardon?"

"She can walk in the sunlight," Gregor said enviously.

"Is that so?"

"The gun didn't even affect her."

"Really?" Skye spun in his chair to eye Bronwyn in interest. "Can I ask how?"

She lifted her chin. "None of your business. I'm not telling the Agency anything more about myself until I know I can trust you."

He sighed, but he nodded. "I understand."

She ignored him. She narrowed her eyes at Remy. She turned to face him squarely. "It will have to wait. You aren't looking good."

They all turned to look at Remy. He scowled and lifted his chin defiantly.

Ah. So, they weren't aware of his deteriorating condition. Interesting. "That blast must have taken a lot out of you," she told him shrewdly.

He looked at her in silence for a moment as if he wasn't sure what he wanted to do with her. She had a good idea of what the options were. Finally, he nodded. "I can show you a place to sleep, if you need to get some rest."

She shrugged. She didn't, but she wouldn't mind a few hours of peace. "Sure."

He tilted his head. She followed him out of the lab and up a winding staircase toward the residence and guest rooms. He didn't speak to her, but she could sense his mind racing wildly. They were only racing on one direction. He paused in front of a door and turned to her. His eyes glittered. For a moment, he stared intently into her eyes as if she might turn on him suddenly and attack. She smirked.

He spun and pushed open the door. The room beyond was featureless and comfortable, like a hotel room. "Here you are," he said in a low voice. "Is this comfortable enough for you?"

She stepped into the room, but she did not move around it to examine its merit. She looked at him. "It's not the Fairmont, but it will do."

He blinked. "Is that where you're staying?"

She smirked.

"No wonder I couldn't find you at the After Dark."

She laughed. "I wouldn't stay at that flophouse."

"I suppose you don't need light-tight rooms."

"No. I'll be fine here. It's very...comfortable. It's not as though I intend to move in."

He nodded. He stared at her silently for a long moment. He didn't move.

She did. She pressed her body against his. He stiffened. She was soft and firm in all the right places. He closed his eyes. He could feel every inch of her. His skin heated. Her breath cooled his neck and ear as she spoke. "Are you waiting for a tip?" He smirked. "Or are you just hoping I'll show you another trick?"

He chuckled. He stepped away from her and strode toward the door. He nodded and pulled it shut without a word. Bronwyn laughed and sat down on the bed. She might not agree with the Agency in general, but they did know how to pick their agents.

Of course, they probably put him to different use than she intended to.

* * *

Bronwyn wasn't wearing the long black coat and pants when she met Remy in the lobby around noon. She'd changed into a shorter black, leather jacket and a skirt so short, it barely covered the curve of her bottom. Her legs were long and well-shaped. Black boots with buttons up the sides ended at her knees. She smirked at him. He blinked at her for several seconds. He decided not to ask how she'd managed to come upon the change of clothes. She might have visited her own hotel without anyone noticing.

It was best not to ask a woman such a question, especially when she could rip out his throat without a moment's hesitation.

He sipped his coffee silently. She lifted her eyebrows. "Do you drink coffee?" he asked finally.

Her full, ruby red lips turned up slightly at the corners. "Yes. I know it's proper for the English to enjoy tea, but I always preferred coffee."

"Then you will be offended by the sludge we make here." He smirked. "Want a cup?"

"Sure."

The coffee station was a small side table on the far side of the lobby near the door. He poured her a Styrofoam cup of the thick, strong coffee from the industrial sized pot. "We drink a lot of coffee here." He inhaled sharply when he turned to find her so close. He had to lift the cup into the air to avoid colliding with her.

She smiled and took it carefully from his fingers. "I can tell." She brushed past him as she moved to the table to empty a single packet of raw sugar into the cup. Her skin was as cold as ice. It soothed the sudden heat that rushed through him. She seemed to sense it. She stepped away from him and sipped the coffee. She did not seem to mind the unnatural consistency or the hellish strength. "Anything new on your scientist?"

He lifted his eyes abruptly from her mouth. "No. Nothing yet. No property records. No one's seen him in a few months. We have a call in to his daughter. She's a lawyer in D.C. She hasn't returned it yet. We'll know more once we've spoken to her."

She nodded. "Right, then. Shall we go?"

He hesitated. "You really can walk in sunlight?"

She rolled her eyes and preceded him to the door. When she stepped outside, he sucked in a nervous breath. She glanced at him. "It's not even sunny."

He chuckled. "How are you doing it?"

She drew a pair of rose-tinted aviators from her jacket pocket and slipped them on. She smirked. "There are things a woman likes to keep private."

He didn't ask again. He doubted she would tell him, anyway.

Bronwyn seemed interested in the scenery on the drive through town. There was no expression on her face, but she stared out the window intently. "Have you been here before?"

She glanced at him. "Yes, but it was a very long time ago. In the early 1900's. It was still very much undeveloped them. It's interesting to see how it's changed."

"You haven't had the opportunity to return in over a hundred years?"

She shrugged. "I've been very busy. My work has not drawn me here in many years."

"You've been doing it the whole time? Hunting creatures?"

"No. Only for the last hundred years."

"You must have seen many things."

"Yes."

"You started with your sire."

She turned in her seat to stare silently at him for several seconds. He wondered if she would reply at all. Finally she said in an utterly toneless voice, "Ah. I wondered when you'd get to that." She smiled and turned back to the scenery flying past the window.

"If it makes you uncomfortable…"

She chuckled low in her throat. "It doesn't make me uncomfortable." She was silent another long moment. He didn't expect her to respond. He was surprised when she did. "I grew up the daughter of a baronet in Regency England. All my life I lived next door to Alys Sayer, my oldest and dearest friend. One day Rafe came to town calling himself His Illustrious Lord Rafael, Count of Toreno." She chuckled bitterly. "He was no such thing. He was the son of a Basque farmer in the 17th century. He drained and killed Alys slowly." She stopped speaking for a few moments. "He was using her to get to me. He used our connection to each other to form a psychic link to me. He seduced me as he seduced her. And when she was dead, I gave him what he wanted and let him turn me into a vampire."

He lifted an eyebrow. "That doesn't seem like the appropriate reaction."

She laughed. "I needed to be strong enough to kill him, to know more about what he was and what his weaknesses were. I needed to be what he was, and I needed him to teach me about being a vampire. I needed him to teach me how to kill him. He taught me many things. He taught me about myself. After a while, I became almost…"

She shrugged. She looked away, and he knew there was something she didn't want to tell him about Rafe. There was something strange in her voice, but Remy thought he knew. He knew the sort of power a sire held over his changelings. "Sire love," he said tonelessly. "It's quite common."

She glanced at him sharply, but she did not reply to this. "When I felt he had taught me all he could, I plotted to end him. He was well protected. I believe he became aware of my plan. He sensed my true feelings toward him. He had gathered a nest, almost an army. They were the most bloodthirsty and ruthless clan of vampires I have since seen. I did not belong with them." She frowned. "I do not need to kill to feed. I was Rafe's favorite. He genuinely loved me, but he knew I wanted him dead.

"One night, he sent one of our nest-mates, a young man named Elias, to my resting place. I was prepared for an attack. I killed Elias, and I killed the others who stood in my way until I reached Rafe, and then I killed him." She sighed. "And then I was free."

He frowned and considered this a long moment. "That's a lot to go through just for revenge."

She narrowed her eyes behind the rose-tinted glasses. "Alys was my only friend. My life was dull and dreadful. I felt as if I would lose my mind. Alys was the only thing I cared about, and he took her from me."

He nodded slowly. "I understand."

He was still thinking about it as he steered the SUV into a space down a dark, quiet alley in the Tenderloin. The buildings surrounding the alley loomed over them and cast them in deep shadow. He looked at Bronwyn's face. There was no expression there. She met his gaze, and he felt a brief, poignant moment of sadness for her. She was alone.

"Can you smell anything?"

She lifted an eyebrow as if she'd known what he'd been thinking. She turned her back to him. "No. Not yet. Let's take a walk."

"Okay."

She walked slowly beside him. She didn't speak for several long moments. Remy suspected she could cover the entire neighborhood in minutes if she wished. She didn't seem to. She seemed to be enjoying the crisp, chilly air. He glanced sidelong at her. Her long, mahogany hair blew out behind her.

"Was it worth it?" he asked suddenly.

She looked at him. She didn't hesitate. "Yes. I believe it was. I had nothing to live for. Now I have a purpose."

"Hunting killers? Saving innocent lives?"

She scowled at him. "You sound cynical. What about you? You do the same."

"I don't have a choice."

"No. You don't, do you?" Now she smiled. "Didn't you do the same thing I do?"

His shoulders stiffened. "What do you know about it?"

"I know more than you think. I have very ample resources." He scowled, but she wasn't deterred. "You're only working for the Agency as punishment for going on a rampage and killing a nest of vampires with a blast of that black juju you used on me."

His voice was low and carefully controlled. "They deserved it. They were evil. They were killing people in droves."

She lifted an eyebrow. "How about that. Doesn't the Agency usually lock your kind up in detox until they can get all the black magic out of you?"

He looked away. "They thought I would be more useful this way. Working for them. They sentenced me to ten years as an agent, but I am free to live my own life otherwise. I took it." His jaw stiffened. "Little did I know the job would become my whole life."

"You worked for *Castus Vox*. How different can it be? You want to destroy evil. Isn't this as good a way as any?"

"It's better than your way, anyway."

She laughed. "Is it?" She stopped moving and stepped into his path. He reared back to avoid colliding with her. "Didn't you want to feel that way yourself? Wouldn't you prefer to be free, to do as you please?" Her voice was a low, sensual purr. She stepped closer as he leaned back away from her, as though her words could poison or burn him. "Doesn't the magic just shiver inside you, begging to be released? You hold so much inside. Don't you just want to let it all out?"

He reached out for her. He seized the back of her head with one hand and molded her body against his with the other. He dipped his head to meet her mouth with his. Her tongue darted out to stroke frantically against his. His body heated, and even her ice cold skin was warm and pliant. He pressed her back against the alley wall. She moaned low and deliberately in her throat and angled her waist so she could feel his erection pressing into her belly.

His hand slid up her bare thigh and under the hem of her skirt. He yanked her thigh up to his hip. His fingertips brushed across the top of the lacy panties her short skirt barely covered. She wasn't cold there. She was as hot and moist as a volcano. He groaned and slipped his fingers under the hem of her panties to seek out her arousal.

She laughed and pushed him away. The throaty, husky sound echoed through the alley. "There now. Wasn't it nice to just let go?" He stared at her in surprise. His tongue flicked against his bared teeth. She stepped forward again and spoke against his mouth. "I can't wait to see what happens when you really let it out, Remy. I can see inside you. I can see what you really want." She brushed a hand across the bulge in his trousers. She leaned back to meet his gaze. "You aren't some monster the Agency wields to do its dirty work. You're a man."

Her voice echoed in his ears as though she was hypnotizing him. She might have been. His arousal pulsed through his body like electricity. He didn't care who could see them or who could be listening from the crumbling tenements around them. His body vibrated against the restraint. She leaned close to his ear. Her breath soothed his heated flesh.

"You want to bend me over in this alley and pound into me until I'm screaming for more. You want to make me come so hard I never think of another man again without wanting him to be you. You want to come inside me and brand me as yours forever."

He growled and advanced upon her. He caught her hips and spun her to face the wall. He pressed an arm against her shoulders to hold her in place and fumbled for his belt. She laughed quietly, but she didn't fight him. "What about what you want?" he demanded against her ear. His breath was harsh and ragged. He lifted her skirt to her waist and dipped his hand into the lace panties. His fingers thrust roughly inside her. She was hot and wet. She arched back against his long, rigid cock as he freed it from his pants. "Is this what you want?"

He didn't wait for her reply. He nudged her legs open with his knee and tugged her panties down. He guided himself to her slit. He pressed his forefinger against her sensitive clit as he drove up inside her tight, inviting depth. She moaned and tossed her head. He caught a fistful of her hair and angled her head back. With the other hand, he gripped her hip to anchor her as he pounded into her. Her feet left the ground with the force of his thrusts. She braced herself against the wall and turned her head so she could see the glittering, intense expression in his brilliant blue eyes. He sank his teeth into the sensitive spot between her neck and shoulders as they moved wildly together.

He worked frantically at her clit until her quim clenched and quivered around him. She cried out and clawed at the wall as an orgasm racked her body. His fingers bit into her skin, bruising and healing in the same instant. Remy moaned and threw his head back. He gripped her shoulder as his thrusts became hard and erratic. Pleasure rolled over him in a shuddering wave. With one final stroke, he came and collapsed against her, pressing her into the wall.

She spun around to face him when he pulled out of her. She adjusted her clothes as though nothing out of the ordinary had happened. Remy caught her into his arms and kissed her. His tongue swept every inch of her mouth, opening it to him as if he meant to taste everything he'd missed. When he pulled away, he leaned his forehead against hers and brushed her hair tenderly back from her face.

He drew back suddenly in surprise and looked down at his hands. They were steady. There was no swirl of black energy or trembling sensation of need. His tanned skin almost glowed. He felt calm and peaceful. He looked at her sharply. "What did you do to me?"

She smiled. "Do you feel better?"

"Yes, actually." He frowned. "Was that what that was? Pity?"

Bronwyn laughed. "Oh, no. It was a reward all its own." She leaned toward him and pressed her lips against his. "Let's get back to work. Maybe when we're done here I can show you how rewarding I can be."

He smirked and caught the back of her head to kiss her more earnestly.

She pulled back. "People are dying."

"Yes, and we're the only ones who can stop it."

"Does that excite you?"

He advanced upon her so her back met the wall again. He lifted her thigh to dip his fingers into her still warm and moist depth. She closed her eyes and mewled softly like a kitten. "I guess it excites you."

"No," she breathed. "That was all you."

He thrust two fingers inside her and worked her clit with the pad of his thumb. "I want to see your face when you come."

She opened her eyes to meet his glittering gaze. She gripped his shoulders to steady herself as he stroked her. With his free hand he kneaded her breasts, squeezing the taut, sensitive nipple through her thin tank top and bra until she gasped and arched into his powerful hands. She let him take her up again on a wave of pleasure, and she cried out as another orgasm swept through her body.

It might have been her heightened vampire senses or she might have always

118

run so hot. Her orgasms were effortless and powerful. When he withdrew from her, she looked at him with a small smile. "I can sniff out the neighborhood more quickly on my own."

"I'm not letting you out of my sight."

She laughed. "You won't have to for long. With you, this will take all day. We have better things to do."

She didn't wait for his assent. She was gone in a flash. His blonde hair blew around his face as if he'd stepped into a sudden gust of wind. She'd told him the truth. She returned to his side in mere minutes. He lifted an eyebrow.

"Done."

"Did you find anything?"

She shook her head. "No. The location is masked somehow. I sense something strange in the air all around us. I can't pinpoint where it's coming from."

"Could it be some kind of magical cloaking?"

"Maybe, but there aren't many magical shields that can fool me."

He narrowed his eyes. "How can you do so much? Is it Cicely?"

She stiffened instantly. "What do you know about Cicely?"

He sensed he was on dangerous ground. "Just that she's a white sorceress in Ireland and has been around a very long time."

Bronwyn nodded, but her expression didn't soften much. "I met her shortly after I killed Rafe and my nest-mates. She found me in a small village near Dublin. She said she saw me in a vision and knew she was meant to help me." She hesitated a moment, but their moments together must have softened her toward him. "She granted me powers other vampires do not possess."

"Like the flying."

"I can't fly."

"What?"

"I can levitate hella high, but I can't fly. That's ridiculous."

"That seems enough like the same thing."

"It isn't. I can shape shift when I need to, and I can walk in the daylight."

Remy lifted an eyebrow. "That was nice of her. Did you grant her eternal life in exchange?"

Bronwyn glanced at him sharply. "I did not turn her, if that's what you are asking. She possesses powers others would kill for it they could. Stay away from her."

"I don't intend to bother her. She's out of my jurisdiction, anyway."

"Good."

"So, about those rewards..."

Bronwyn laughed. "Let me drive."

 CHAPTER FIVE

Remy hung on for dear life. Bronwyn stamped down on the brakes. The SUV screeched to a halt on the street outside the Agency headquarters. The drive had been harrowing. She was a fast driver. She was a reckless driver. Her reflexes were so fast, it didn't matter. Remy felt as though he'd just been tossed into a cement mixer and shaken up for a few minutes until his brain was scrambled and his body felt like jelly.

"I thought we were going to your hotel."

Bronwyn glanced at him. "What kind of girl do you think I am?"

He snorted.

She narrowed her eyes. "We're working a case. We need to find out if there's any new information on your scientist. If we discover who he is, I might be able to catch his scent somehow. The mixed up monsters might not be giving off a definable scent, but a human certainly will." She leaned toward him. "You're the easiest to smell."

"Are we?"

"Of course. You have life. Vitality. Blood."

He considered. "All right. It doesn't sound like a bad idea. It's the best we've got."

Skye and Fallon glanced up at them as they entered the laboratory side by side. Skye's expression did not change, but he stared at them for a long, silent moment. Fallon's jaw set. She turned away from them to peer at her screen. Her fingers did not move over the console. Bronwyn glanced at Remy. He took a step closer to her as if to confirm his co-workers suspicions. They knew.

"Did you discover anything?" Skye asked into the charged silence.

Fallon half turned her head. Her eyes were bloodshot. She looked as if she hadn't slept in days. She might have been crying. "No," Remy replied.

"I was unable to sniff out any sign of the lab."

Skye pushed his glasses up on the bridge of his nose. "Could some sort of spell be masking the lab from us?"

"It could be, but it would have to be a pretty powerful spell. I'm an old vampire. My senses are highly developed. I can sniff out anything."

Skye nodded. "I'll look into what it could be."

Bronwyn cocked her head to the side to study him. "Is that all you do? Research?"

There was no inflection in her voice, but Skye stiffened. "I'll have you know, I am the boss of this place."

"Ah."

"I used to be a field agent."

"I understand." She moved closer to him like a jungle cat stalking its prey.

"I was injured."

Fallon spun in her chair to glare at Bronwyn. "Skye is good at what he does. He can uncover anything."

Bronwyn's eyes flicked to her. "I'm sure he can. What about you? Are you useful to the operation in your condition?"

Remy and Skye exchanged an uneasy glance. Fallon shot out of her seat to face the taller vampire squarely. She glared. "I don't know what that's supposed to mean."

"Don't you?" Bronwyn smiled. She stepped back from Fallon. "It's hard to control all that power and anger, isn't it?" Fallon's eyes darkened as though her pupils were dilating. "You need a little help now and again."

Above her head, the florescent light exploded. It showered them in a spray of tiny shards of glass. "Fallon!" Remy barked.

"Calm down, psychic."

"You don't belong here," Fallon hissed. "You're one of them. One of the things we hunt. You're just a soulless, dead thing."

Bronwyn smiled.

"Fallon!" Remy's voice was harsh.

Fallon spun on him with burning eyes. "And you. You disgust me." She turned away from him and raced out of the room. Her footsteps echoed up the stairs to her bedroom.

"Sorry," Bronwyn said. She didn't sound very sorry. "I didn't mean to rile her up."

"Yes, you did," Skye said.

"She's hanging by a thread, you know. You ought to do something about her."

He rose. "This is my duty station. I do not allow outsiders to give me advice about how to run it."

She chuckled. "You humans are so sensitive."

Remy smirked slightly as though he was enjoying the tension. Skye scowled at him. "If there's nothing else, I have some research to do. We do have a job here."

Remy caught Bronwyn's hand and tugged her out of the room toward the bedrooms. "You sure know how to make friends," he remarked as he closed his bedroom door behind him.

"I'm not trying to make friends."

"So you had some other reason for stirring up everyone in the office?"

She laughed. "It's fun."

"That's not very nice."

"I'm not a very nice girl. Do you have a problem with it?"

He smirked. "I'm not a very nice guy." He snaked an arm around her waist and yanked her up against him. "And I don't care who knows it."

She lifted her head to meet his kiss. His tongue plunged insistently into her mouth. She sighed and melted into his kiss. She wrapped her arms around his neck, but he caught them and pushed them off. He shoved her black leather jacket from her shoulders and tugged on the hem of her tank top. He broke the kiss for a split second to lift it over her head. Her skin was cool like marble. It was soft and pliable under his fingers as they stroked across her abdomen and up to cup her breasts through her bra. She sighed. He reached behind her to unfasten her bra with nimble fingers.

He caught her shoulders and held her away from him. Her eyes burned into his. Her mouth was parted slightly. Her tongue flicked across her sharp teeth. Remy met her gaze as he stroked her bare breasts. Her skin was milky white, but her nipples were taut and as pink as petals. He rolled them between his fingertips. She tossed her head back and arched toward him. She moved closer to him and reached for the buttons on his shirt.

Remy batted her hands away. He caught her abruptly around the waist and spun her around to toss her back onto the bed. Her eyes clouded over with lust as she watched him move slowly toward the bed. His hands slid up her long legs. He caught the hem of her skirt and tugged it down. He paused to peer at her with glittering eyes.

"Remy."

Her voice was a soft, insistent purr. If she was mesmerizing him, it was working. He ignored her. "Take off your panties."

She lifted an eyebrow. "Why don't you do it?"

"I told you to do it."

Bronwyn's mouth turned up slightly at the corners, but she did not refuse. She stood and shimmied out of her panties, kicking them away. She moved toward him to press her mouth to his, but he pushed her back down to the bed and stood over her. "Come to me, Remy."

Now she was mesmerizing him. His body throbbed and tightened, but he fought her hold on him. He unbuttoned his shirt rapidly and shrugged it off his shoulders. Her eyes followed his movements. His flat, lean muscles rippled. She looked as though she was undecided whether to make love to him or sink her teeth into the hard, tanned flesh of his broad shoulders. Her gaze seemed to trace down the veins pumping blood through his body. It settled upon the bulge in his jeans. She smiled.

She lifted herself onto her elbows and opened her legs to him. He stared at her long, lean naked body. Her breasts were full and rounded with pert, taut nipples. She didn't need to breathe, but they heaved nevertheless. Her waist tapered into the curve of her hips. A light patch of hair tapered toward the smooth, slick folds of her swollen quim.

He moved toward her and gripped her ankles to push her knees up to her chest. She dragged herself backward on her elbows to allow him onto the bed, but he didn't move atop her. He dipped his head to kiss the inside of her thigh. Her muscles quivered with the anticipation of his touch. He stroked a finger along the folds of her quim. She tossed her head back and moaned low in her throat. He spread her velvety folds with two fingers and pressed his thumb against the swollen, sensitive nub.

He leaned down and stroked her clit with the flat of his tongue. His mouth was hot and searing. She gasped as he swirled his tongue around the throbbing nub. Pleasure built with each stroke and suckle. She reached down to clutch at his head. He shoved her hands away and hooked them under her legs. He palmed her breasts in his large, strong hands. She arched her hips. He pinched her nipples between his fingers.

She moved restlessly against his mouth. When his hands left her breasts she whimpered in protest. He ignored her. Without unsealing his mouth from her quim, he plunged a finger inside her. She cried out. Pleasure built up inside her. She clutched at the rumpled counterpane. Her thighs trembled.

He felt her muscles contract around his finger. As soon as her orgasm began, he pulled away from her abruptly. She gasped and exhaled heavily. She looked at him in surprise, but he was already kicking away his pants. His rigid cock slapped against his belly. He was upon her so quickly, her quim convulsed around his cock as he plunged inside her. She tossed her head back and cried out.

Remy gripped her knee and tugged her hips up to thrust more deeply inside her. She called out his name as an orgasm broke upon her like a tidal wave. His hand skimmed roughly over her breasts. He squeezed her sensitive nipples. Her body rocked with his as he pounded forcefully into her. He bared his teeth and growled low in his throat as pleasure rolled over him. His fingers tightened on her thigh and breasts, and she cried out as the pain heightened the pleasure crashing over her.

Remy met her glittering eyes and shouted out as he came inside her. He stroked inside her more slowly as her quim contracted and tiny, lingering shockwaves of pleasure shivered through his body. He panted as he pulled out of her. She whimpered softly as she dropped limply back on the bed. He fell onto his back beside her.

Remy wrapped an arm around her waist and drew her up against his side. He was silent for several long moments. She leaned her head against his chest and listened to the quick, powerful thumping of his heart. Her heart didn't race. Her heart didn't beat.

"I always wondered how vampires still have sex."

Bronwyn lifted her head to look at him in surprise. "What are you talking about?"

He stroked her wet quim languidly. It was still swollen and sensitive. She sighed. "You get so wet. It defies the laws of nature."

She laughed. "That's really what you're thinking about right now?"

He pushed her shoulder back to lean over her. He dipped his head and licked her nipple. He nipped it gently with his teeth. "Not exactly. It just occurred to me."

"Vampires defy the laws of nature. I don't know how it works; it just does."

"Yes, it does. It definitely does." He suckled her nipple. His hand slid down to rub her clit.

Bronwyn batted him away. "Don't start something you can't finish. Vampires don't need time to replenish themselves like humans."

Remy lifted his eyebrows and smirked. "Neither do I." He caught her hand and shoved it down to his cock. It was still hard and hot. She stroked it. He groaned. "I want to be inside you again. Right now."

"You do need time, even if you think you don't." She released him and laid back on the pillows. She pushed him off her. She was stronger than him. She'd submitted to him before, but she could have tossed him aside as easily as a rag doll. He could not take her in any way she did not choose to be taken.

He sighed. She was probably right. His hands weren't shaking. There was no black magic swirling around him, but his heart still pounded rapidly in his chest. She lifted a hand and gently brushed his blonde hair from his eyes. Her touch was so soft and tender, he closed his eyes for the briefest moment.

He hadn't realized he'd fallen asleep until he awoke with a start. Bronwyn was awake. She met his startled gaze. "How long was I asleep?"

"Not long. About twenty minutes."

"What did you do to me?"

"Nothing."

He frowned. "Nothing?"

She lifted her eyebrows. "I did not put you under a spell, if that's what you mean."

He shook his head. "No. Sorry. I didn't mean--I've never felt that relaxed before. Not that I could remember."

She smiled. "You are satisfied."

"It's more than that." He stared at her in silence for several long moments, then he leaned toward her to press his mouth against hers. She flicked out her tongue, and he caught it with his own, suckling it gently. He brushed her long, dark auburn hair from her shoulders and rolled atop her, nudging her knees apart. His cock rubbed against her thigh.

"Remy." She broke the kiss. She smiled and stroked his hair gently.

126

"I want you, Bronwyn."

"I know." She sucked in a breath as he flicked his fingers over her nipples.

He gripped his cock to guide it inside her. She sat up suddenly. He sighed, but he drew back. "All right, I can take a hint."

She smiled. "You can have me again. Just not right now."

"All right. What would you like to do instead?"

She laughed. "You say it as if there is nothing else."

"We could play cards. I think I have a deck somewhere."

She rolled her eyes. "Or we could talk to each other."

"Novel."

"Are you only interested in my body?'

He considered this seriously. He sat up to lean against the headboard beside her. "Okay. Let's talk to each other."

For a long moment, she was silent. She glanced at him through the veil of her long, tousled hair, then she leaned back against the headboard beside him. "Do you miss the *Castus Vox*?"

He blinked. He glanced at her. "Really? This is what we're doing?"

"Why not?"

He shrugged. "Sure. Let's get to know each other better." He thought about her question for several long moments. Finally, he glanced at her. His dark blonde hair fell over his forehead, making him look almost vulnerable as he replied, "I shouldn't. Their guidelines are strict. They see the world in black and white, good and evil." He sighed. He smiled at her as she brushed the stray lock of hair out of his eyes. "Not everyone can be that way."

Bronwyn frowned. "In my experience, none of them are."

He ignored this. "I grew up in the order. My father, Alain and mother, Elizabeth, were in the order. I was born into it. I lived in the compound all my life. My parents died in the service. I would have died there, too, if I hadn't been turned out."

"Did you ever think it was best?"

"Yes. All the time. It doesn't change that they were my family."

She nodded. "Will you try to go back, when your sentence is over?"

"There's no going back."

"What if you could?"

He shook his head. "I don't think about that. I think about the future."

"So what's in the future?"

He sighed and leaned back against the headboard. "I don't know. In five years, my sentence is over."

"I have read your file. They would let you stay on here."

"You read my file?"

She chuckled. "I have many resources."

He decided not to pursue this. "I'm not sure I want to stay on."

"What will you do instead?"

This was an uncomfortable question. Remy thought about it. "I've been fighting evil all my life. Maybe I'll take a holiday. One where there are no creatures. Someone else can do the fighting for once."

She chuckled and moved down to lay back on the pillows.

Remy slid down beside her and propped himself up to lean over her. He kissed her. His hand slid down over her naked body. She sighed as he stroked her breasts. "Maybe you can come with me."

"I thought you said no creatures."

"You aren't a creature."

"No? What am I then?"

He slid down her body and licked her nipples. He sucked one into his mouth, nipped it gently with his teeth. He lifted his head to look at her. "A hostile."

Her laugh ended in a moan as he swirled his tongue around her nipple and slid a finger abruptly inside her. "Aren't you worried about what the others think?"

"Why would I be?" He rubbed her clit with his thumb as he stroked his finger inside her.

She sighed and tangled her fingers into his dark blonde hair. "They're your co-workers."

"So?"

"They're not also your friends?"

128

He considered this as he attacked her other nipple with his tongue. He caressed her soft, taut abdomen with his free hand. His mouth vibrated against her sensitive flesh. "I'm not sure I would call them friends."

She arched into him. "Do you call anyone a friend?"

Remy lifted his head to look at her. "What about you?"

She glanced away. Her expression was dark. "Yes."

He sighed and dropped a kiss on her belly. "I'm sorry. I shouldn't have said that." He sighed. "No, I don't have anyone I care so much about I would get myself turned into a vampire just to wait a hundred years to take revenge."

She smirked. "Not many people do."

He braced himself above her and leaned down to press his mouth to hers. He cupped the sides of her face in his hands. His tongue stroked languidly against hers. She sighed softly and wrapped her arms around his neck. His cock pressed against her thigh, but he didn't move to thrust inside her. He lifted his head to look into her face. "I'm willing to learn what it's like to feel that way about someone."

She lifted an eyebrow. "We met yesterday."

His expression was deadly serious. His brilliant blue eyes bore into hers. "I've never felt this way before."

She sighed and looked away. He tilted her chin to bring her gaze back to his. "Have you ever been with a vamp?"

He blinked. "No."

"Well, there you are. Don't make more out of it than it is."

He frowned. "It is more."

"You feel that way now. Don't worry. When I'm gone, it will fade."

He stared down at her. "I don't think so."

She smiled slightly and lifted her head to kiss him. Her hands stroked over his hard, muscled behind and around to cup his balls in her hand. He groaned softly and she gripped his rigid cock in her hand, guiding it toward her moist, swollen opening. He didn't thrust inside her. He caught her face in his hands. There was determination in his eyes. Her thrall was powerful, but he was trained to shrug off its effects.

She didn't argue with him, despite the doubt in her eyes. He frowned. "Are you saying you're going to leave when this is over?"

"It's what I do." She gasped as he slid his cock slowly inside her. Her voice was slightly strangled. "I move around, follow the job."

He pulled completely out of her, then pushed back inside. His balls slapped against her as he buried himself as deeply as he could go. She moaned. He stroked slowly inside her. His eyes bore into hers. "Will you come back?"

She didn't answer for a long moment. She threw her head back and angled her hips up to meet him.

"Bronwyn, will you come back?"

"I don't want to give you false hope."

He stopped moving and frowned. "Bronwyn."

She sighed. "Maybe. I don't know."

Remy kissed her. "I want you to take me."

She blinked at him. "What?"

He tilted his head to reveal his throat. Blood pumped through his veins. Her mouth opened, and she flicked her tongue over her lip. "Do it, Bronwyn."

Her eyes snapped back to his. He looked serious. Blood lust swept through her. She moved so suddenly, he didn't realize she'd flipped him until she landed atop him, tossing her head back as she lowered herself onto his cock. Her long, auburn hair swept his legs as she rocked forward and back on him. He gripped her hips and rose up to suckle her nipples. She rode him until her quim quivered and tightened around him. She lowered her head to look at him.

She pushed him back down to the pillows and struck like a snake, sinking her fangs into the soft flesh between his neck and shoulder. Blood leaked from her lips and trickled down onto the pale blue pillowcase. Remy didn't care. He cried out and gripped her hips, thrusting wildly up into her as the blood moved rapidly from his veins into her mouth. The sensation was strange. His body felt light, as if he was suddenly floating, but his cock tightened painfully. Pleasure rolled slowly over him, building up as intensely as his dark magic until it exploded inside her like a blast of energy.

She lifted slightly off the bed as if he had shocked her. She jerked her head from his neck, licking the droplets of blood from her lips as she tossed back her head. She moaned as she rode out their simultaneous orgasms. Her quim quivered around his cock as if she meant to draw the last drop of his life from it.

He didn't feel weak as she collapsed beside him. He felt light and peaceful, as if he hadn't a care in the world. Endorphins rushed through him. His eyes felt heavy. He lifted his head laboriously to kiss her. Her lips tasted faintly coppery from his blood. She panted as she looked back at him from under hooded eyes. She looked almost rosy.

"Maybe I can convince you to stay." His voice was a low, husky murmur. "Or at least come back."

She smiled languidly. "You're getting a pretty good start on that."

He didn't hear her reply. Darkness swirled up around him and sucked him under.

CHAPTER SIX

The room was dark when Remy awoke beside Bronwyn. She was still asleep. Her long, red hair fanned out over his pillows. Her chest did not rise and fall as she breathed. She wasn't breathing. If he didn't know what she was, he would have feared she'd died in her sleep. She looked peaceful. Her color was better. His blood was strong and powerful. She looked almost human. She was beautiful. He stroked a hand down her back.

She opened her eyes slowly. Her lips curled up, and she arched her back slightly. Her sculpted, ivory pale behind rise. He dragged his tongue across his teeth. He considered mounting her and spreading her open as he made love to her from behind. She seemed to catch the train of his thoughts. Her eyes dropped to his half-erect cock.

She sat up and drew the counterpane up to her chest to hide her breasts from his burning eyes. "Dusk is falling," she said in a low voice.

He sighed. "Yeah. All right. We'd better go see what's happening with the others. They might have learned something."

Fallon wasn't in the lab when they walked inside. Noah and Gregor looked up at them as they entered. Gregor shot to his feet. His fangs protracted suddenly. He was beside Remy in a flash with his teeth bared. Remy blinked in surprise. Bronwyn moved so quickly, he felt his hair blow back as she stood between him and Gregor. She bared her fangs and hissed at Gregor.

"Whoa!" Noah exclaimed, shooting to his feet. "What the hell, man?"

Gregor seemed to come to his senses. He passed a hand over his face. When he looked back around at them, his fangs retracted. He stepped away from Bronwyn. "I'm sorry. I--I smelled blood."

Bronwyn's fangs retracted, but her muscles remained coiled to strike. "Get it together."

Gregor stepped back. "Sorry, Rem. You just smell--" He spun away and sank into his chair.

Skye peered at them over the top of his glasses. "Can we please stay focused here?"

They all turned to look at him. Remy gestured Bronwyn into the chair in front of his console and sat at Fallon's station. "What have we got?"

Skye sighed. He jerked his head toward his monitor. "I can't figure out how he's shielding the lab from us. It could be any one of the spells in the Agency's database. It could be something else." Bronwyn's eyes moved rapidly back and forth as she read the search results on Skye's screen. "We could try some of these counter spells. It would at least eliminate what he isn't using."

"That could work," Remy said thoughtfully.

Bronwyn frowned. "I prefer to have an actual direction, rather than a series of failures."

"We would all like to work with more," Skye said with a slight edge in his voice.

"Have you heard anything about Dr. Fisk?" Remy asked.

"No. His daughter hasn't returned any of our calls."

Remy sighed. "All right. Give me the counter spells and we can try them."

"Perhaps we should move the search outward, into the surrounding neighborhoods," Noah said.

Gregor shook his head. "We already have done. I've sent some other vamps out to canvas the surrounding areas."

Bronwyn glanced at him with lifted eyebrows. "Have you?"

He frowned. "I'm not a complete idiot. I know how to outsource. With someone in every neighborhood, we covered it all in a short time. No one has been able to smell anything. There's nothing to smell. It's why they thought the missing vamps were dead. They can't smell them anymore. There's no hint of them."

"They might have left," Bronwyn said. She didn't sound as if she believed it.

Gregor shook his head. "Not that many. Not without saying a word to anyone. You know how the community is. Someone always knows."

"So what do we do?" Noah asked, squaring his shoulders.

"Patrol," Remy suggested. "It's all we've got right now."

"I have some volunteers patrolling the other neighborhoods when night falls," Gregor added. "We can work the Tenderloin where the attacks have occurred and where Noah last saw the creature."

"With Gregor and Bronwyn, we might have a better chance of capturing it,"

Skye said. "It is a hybrid of intelligent creatures. It might be able to talk to us. It might even turn on its creator and give us something."

They all considered this. "For the sake of the investigation," Remy said darkly, "I hope so. But for the sake of the ones who've been spliced, I hope they aren't intelligent and have no idea what's being done to them. It would be far kinder. We don't actually know what the scientist is doing to create them."

Gregor and Bronwyn shivered involuntarily as though they were sharing their horror. They might have been. Remy glanced at Bronwyn. She lifted her chin. "I want to find him."

Remy nodded. He looked around at the others. "So do I. Bronwyn and I will patrol together. Greg and Noah, you two stay together. I don't want any more attacks, and I don't want the creature to get away this time."

Gregor nodded. "If any of us catch sight of the creature, Bronwyn and I can reach each other and be there to stop it."

Skye waved his hand. "Stop talking about it, then, and get going."

Bronwyn didn't talk to Remy as they strolled through the streets of the Tenderloin. They avoided the noisy, pulsating nightlife. They wound slowly through the dark, empty alleyways. No one was wandering the deserted, lonely streets. Even the vagrants knew that something wasn't right in the city.

They didn't discuss their earlier conversation. They didn't slip into an alley to rekindle their lust. Bronwyn's expression was alert and resolute. Remy didn't try to distract her. His eyes darted warily back and forth. The instruments were silent.

An hour passed. Finally, Bronwyn paused. They stood in a dark, quiet alley. Debris swirled in the slight breeze around their feet. She looked at Remy. He wasn't sure what he expected her to say. He stepped closer to her. Her dark eyes burned. "Tell me what your psychic saw. Why did she think I was involved in this?"

He wasn't sure if she was upset. Her sculpted, marble pale face was expressionless. "She said she saw you surrounded by body parts. She saw you kill a human man."

Bronwyn considered this. "It could be the scientist"

He frowned. "I hope it is."

She rolled her eyes, but she didn't say anything. "Are her visions reliable?"

"They're vivid. They're usually trustworthy."

She lifted an eyebrow as though she read the slight unease in his eyes. "But the interpretation is where it falls apart?"

His mouth turned up slightly into as smirk. "There is room for improvement."

"Yes, I can see that." She stared at him a moment. "Fallon sees more than she lets on."

He frowned. "What are you talking about?"

"She sees things she doesn't share with you. Things about you."

"What do you mean?"

"Things about you...and me."

For a moment, he stared at her. Then he understood. "Oh. I see."

"So I find him."

He blinked.

"The scientist."

"We find him."

She lifted an eyebrow. She didn't say anything to this, but she glanced sideways at him.

He frowned. "Are you thinking of abandoning the Agency?"

She considered this. "Not exactly. I'm just wondering if I do. It's only me in the vision, isn't it?"

Remy nodded slowly. "There was more to the vision, but she couldn't see it all. Sometimes it's like tunnel vision. We don't always get the full picture or understand what it means."

Bronwyn nodded. "It is the way with such a gift. I could see things sometimes when I was human. Not many things, and I didn't understand it then, but it was that which allowed Rafe to get to me, to project images into my head and draw me to him while he hurt Alys." She turned her back to him, and when she spoke again, her voice was soft and toneless. "He enjoyed playing with me. I was so much more than human."

"Do you miss him?"

She spun back to meet his gaze. "Sometimes I think of him, in my darker hours. Sometimes I remember the way he could make me feel."

Remy scowled. "I'm not sure I want to know."

"It was his power. It was all his power. Even after I was vamped, I could not resist his allure. It is a wonder I was able to throw it off to kill him."

"You must have a very strong will."

She lifted her chin. "I have a very strong spirit of vengeance."

"I don't think that's true. Your capacity to love is stronger than your urge to kill."

Her lips turned up slightly. "Is that what you want to believe?"

"I believe it's the truth." He stepped closer to her. "You aren't fooling me, Bronwyn. I see what you really are."

She stiffened. "You don't know anything about me."

"I have seen your eyes when you're on the edge. I've seen you come. I know what you're like when you let go. When you're with me." He wrapped an arm around her waist and tugged her up against him. "I know what you really are."

She frowned, but she didn't step away from him. She held his gaze. He understood her. She liked being with him. She liked being free and uninhibited. She liked giving up her power to him, being dominated and possessed. She liked not having to hide herself from him. When they were together, there was nothing else in the world.

Bronwyn shook her head, and now there was a deep, dark look in her eyes. It was almost grief. It was almost pity. "Don't fool yourself, Remy," she whispered. "I am still what I am. I will not change so easily after one night with a man."

He smirked. He fisted his hand into the hair at the nape of her neck. He spoke against her lips. "I don't believe that, either. I've changed myself after one day with you."

"You haven't. You just think you have."

Remy leaned back to look at her. "If I convinced you my feelings are sincere, would it make a difference?"

She considered this seriously. "I'm not sure. I don't think so...Maybe."

He smiled. 'That's good enough."

A scream rent the air around them. They broke apart instantly and raced toward it. Bronwyn was faster. She was already in front of the creature before Remy reached her three streets away.

He stared at it in horror. It was not larger than a man, but it was burlier. Its features were obscured by the matte of thick, tangled patches of hair on its body. It wasn't wearing clothes, but a tattered rag covered its waist. The hairless patches were marble pale and scaly like a reptile. It shimmered with a horrible, mad light as if its aura had twisted and expanded around it. It bared its teeth at Bronwyn. They were long and sharp. A thin, forked tongue snaked out from its leering maw.

Bronwyn shouted something at it. Remy couldn't understand what she'd said. It sounded odd and ancient and lilting. He'd never heard it before, not in the *Castus Vox* and not at the Agency. It might have been some sort of spell, or it might have been the way vampires communicated, a language that existed in the memories of their blood. When she spoke to it, the creature paused. Its eyes flashed. They were blue like the sky. For a moment, they looked intelligent and alert.

It screamed out again, and this time the sound was anguished and terrified. It pierced through Remy like a blade through his heart.

The creature stared at Bronwyn for several seconds. Then it crouched and rushed suddenly toward her. She cried out again in that strange, melodic language. She sounded almost afraid. Remy spun toward her, to drag her out of the creature's path, but she shoved him away. He bounced against the alley wall.

She tumbled backward as the creature pounced on her. They struggled, snapping at each other with their teeth and flailing their limbs like two drunks in a bar brawl. Drunks typically didn't try to bite each other, at least not in normal bars. Remy rushed toward them, pulling his gun.

"Stay away!" Bronwyn barked. Her voice sounded ragged. She wasn't coming out on top of the fight. She tried to kick her leg over, to flip the creature beneath her, but its long, forked tongue struck out.

It opened a long, thin gash in her cheek as it licked her.

Bronwyn did not shout or cry out. Her movements slowed. Remy could see her head begin to loll. Her eyes looked strange and dreamy. She didn't even fight as the creature bared its fangs and bent down toward her throat.

"Bronwyn!" He rushed toward her, but Gregor stepped into his path, appearing out of the shadows of the night as though he'd heard Bronwyn's call. He probably had. His eyes glowed, and his fangs glistened. He seemed unsure whether or not to dart into the melee.

Gunfire exploded nearby. Remy snapped his head to Noah. He was firing upon the creature with a gun so large, it looked like a cannon. The creature yelped and lifted its head from Bronwyn's throat. She didn't move or struggle. Her dark eyes were open, but there was no life or vitality in them. She didn't look around or meet Remy's gaze.

"Gregor!" Noah barked.

The creature reared back from Bronwyn and leapt to its feet. It ran at full speed toward Remy. Gregor shoved him out of the way, back against the crumbling brick wall. Noah shouted at them and raced after the creature. Gregor didn't wait for Remy. He disappeared in a blur. Remy didn't follow them. He lunged toward Bronwyn.

She didn't stir as he bent over her and brushed her tangled hair from her eyes. She was as cold and silent as death. Two bloody gashes stood out on her starkly pale throat. The creature's tongue left a burn on the side of her cheek. Her wounds weren't healing. She had no pulse, but she hadn't had a pulse in two hundred years. Remy lifted her carefully into his arms and carried her to the SUV. He laid her gently on the backseat.

He heard Gregor and Noah shouting several streets away. He ignored them. He could hear his heart pounding in his ears. He peeled out into the streets and raced back toward headquarters. Bronwyn did not awaken on the drive. He shouted for Skye as he burst through the door. Skye was already in the lobby. He hurried toward Remy with a scowl, but he did not reach out to take Bronwyn from his arms. He lifted his hands uncertainly as if he were warding Remy off.

"What happened?"

"Our patchwork creature." Remy peered down at Bronwyn's face. "It licked her."

"I'm sorry?"

"It licked her. It must be how it transmits its venom. She just stopped fighting. It bit her."

"I can see that." Skye took a hesitant step toward them and brushed Bronwyn's long, tangled red hair to peer more closely at the wound. "She seems to be okay."

"She's not dead?" Remy's voice was tight and breathless.

"Yes, she is, but she's still undead. She will revive and quickly, I suspect. She is very powerful." Skye stepped back from them. "Bring her to bed. She will recover."

"Does she need blood?"

Skye considered. "It might not be a bad idea. It would speed her recovery. I'll get some."

Remy looked down at Bronwyn. She didn't move. Her body was like a block of ice. He shivered slightly, but he hugged her closer to his chest. She would make it. Noah had survived the monster, and he was a human. Bronwyn Liddle was a two hundred year old vampire. She was resilient. She had to be.

He took a hitching breath and looked up at Skye as he strode back into the room with a bag of blood. They didn't need it often, but Skye kept a small supply for emergency situations. Gregor preferred fresh blood from willing victims, but they weren't always practical, especially in the field. The rest of the Secret Service agents preferred not to be the fresh willing donors.

Remy looked away as Skye fed the tube into Bronwyn's mouth. Skye wasn't squeamish. He waited patiently for her to drink. When she had, her body seemed to come alive in Remy's arms. She gasped, though she needed no air to breath. She pushed the bag of blood away. Skye stepped back from her as though he expected her to attack now that she'd tasted blood. She didn't.

Bronwyn rolled her eyes up at Remy. He sighed in relief. She looked weary and weak, but there was some life in her eyes. "She'll be fine," Skye said impassively. "She just needs to revive. She needs time."

Remy didn't glance up at him. He stared down into Bronwyn's face. He felt as though the tightness in his chest had suddenly loosened. He took a deep, steadying breath and nodded. She started slightly in his arms as the door burst open behind them.

Noah and Gregor stomped into the room with slumped shoulders. They looked ragged and windswept, as though they'd braved a fierce storm. Gregor's sculpted face was unmarked, but there were some scratches on Noah's rugged cheeks. He looked better than he had the last time he'd tangled with the patchwork monster.

Gregor strode toward Remy and Bronwyn. "Is she all right?"

"She'll be fine. Did you catch it?"

Noah scowled. "No. It was too fast."

"Even for Gregor?" Skye asked.

Gregor's brow furrowed. "Yes. It outran me easily. I've never seen anything move so fast."

"Perhaps Bronwyn can tell us something more when she awakens. She might have noticed something while she was so close to it."

"I don't think she had time to study it," Remy replied.

"She did," Gregor said darkly. "The only way to learn about a creature is to fight it."

Remy nodded. "I'm taking her upstairs to rest. You can question her later."

* * *

Bronwyn opened her eyes slowly. Pale dawn light filtered in through the dark curtains in Remy's bedroom. She could hear his heart beat, could feel the heat radiating from him before she felt his weight in the bed beside her. Her body felt strong and powerful. She touched her cheek. The wound was gone. Her throat was whole and healed. There was no blood, and she wasn't wearing any clothes. Remy must have cleaned her up.

She turned over to peer at him. His brilliant blue eyes were closed. His dark lashes made shadowed black half-moons on his high cheekbones. She smiled. His chin-length, dark blonde hair fell roguishly into his eyes. He was large and strong, but he looked peaceful and young in sleep. He was as beautiful as a master's sculpture, like a Greek god or a seraph. She reached over and brushed his hair from his eyes. She trailed her hand along his cheek and down to his thick, muscled throat.

He reached for her before he opened his eyes. He drew her body against his. He was naked, and the flat, firm muscles of his form molded against her soft, accommodating flesh. She felt his cock begin to stiffen as it pressed into her bare belly.

She smiled as he opened his eyes. She knew they needed to deal with the patchwork monster and its depraved creator, but she didn't care just then. Arousal pulsed through her. She wanted to feel him inside her again, to draw his strength as he thrust inside her. She wanted to come and feel the heat of his seed pumping into her body as he climaxed.

Remy brushed her hair from her eyes. His hand slid down, over her shoulders and down to cup her full naked breasts. His cock pulsed against her. She leaned closer to him and kissed him. He responded so enthusiastically, thrusting his tongue into her mouth that her cold, undead body heated against his searing flesh. He caught her around the waist and yanked her up to straddle him.

His hands covered her breasts. He pinched her nipples as he kissed her. He bucked up against her. She was wet and warm, and she reached down to guide his thick, stiff cock inside her. She swiveled her hips back to take the length of him inside her. He grunted and lifted his hips to push more deeply inside her. She moved on him, bracing her hands on his chest as she rode his cock. He tore his mouth from hers and fastened his mouth to her nipple, suckling as he gripped her bottom.

She didn't allow him to take control of their movements. She rotated her hips frantically as pleasure built up in her belly, spreading through her body. Her quim tightened and pulsed. He grunted against her breasts. Her orgasm exploded through her body, and she tossed her head back, moaning low in her throat.

Remy rose up abruptly to a sitting position and seized her hips. He moved her against him to meet his thrusts. Curls of pleasure crashed over her as a second orgasm ripped through her. He shouted out his own pleasure as he came suddenly inside her.

He hugged her tightly to him, and she wrapped her arms around his neck. She listened as his heart beat slowly returned to normal, as his breathing settled down. His cock softened inside her. Finally, he leaned back to look at her. His eyes were searching, not lustful. He stared into her face for several seconds. "You're all right? You're feeling better?"

She smiled. "I'm a vampire. I heal remarkably quickly."

He brushed her hair from her face. He kissed her softly, gently on the mouth. "You're sure?"

Bronwyn rolled her eyes. "I'm fine. I feel amazing." She lifted herself off of him and sat back against the headboard. "Did they catch the creature?"

He shook his head and settled back beside her. He took her hand and held it in his lap. "No. It was too fast."

She sighed. "It was so strong. Like nothing I've ever fought before."

"What did it do to you? It licked you?"

She nodded. "Yes. It licked me. The venom had some sort of numbing affect. I could feel my limbs grow heavy. I couldn't move or fight it." She frowned and thought about it for a second. "We've been working this from the vamp/dog angle, but what about the demons? Where's he getting them? How is he trapping them?"

Remy considered. "They're not roaming the streets like the vamps and wolves. Most of the rift openings they come through are monitored. They're accounted for and stopped right away."

"So, how is he getting demons? And enough to experiment on?"

"Good question." He sighed. "We'd better talk to the others."

Bronwyn leaned over and kissed him. He tangled his hand into the hair at the nape of her neck and plunged his tongue inside her mouth. She smiled, but she pressed a hand to his chest to push him away. "We'd better get dressed."

"Yeah, all right. But we'll finish this later."

His tone left no room for argument. She smirked, but she didn't reply. She rose from the bed. In a blur of movement, she darted out of the bedroom. Remy was still blinking in surprise when she returned, fully dressed.

"Where are you getting those clothes?" he demanded, eyeing the tight black pants and black leather jacket she wore.

Bronwyn smiled. "I brought a few things from home."

"When did you have the time?"

"I'm a vampire. I have nothing but time. And I can move very quickly."

He seemed to decide he didn't want to pursue this. He nodded and rose. She perched on the edge of the bed to watch him dress. He stretched languidly. Her eyes lingered on the tight, muscular lines of his back and bottom. His muscles flexed as he moved. If she had a pulse, it would have raced. Her quim heated. She flicked her tongue across her teeth as her fangs protracted slightly.

Remy turned to her with a smirk. She didn't meet his eyes. Her gaze drifted down his firm chest to his tight abs. His cock was already stiffening again. It jutted out of the soft patch of blonde curls at the apex of his V-shaped torso. She didn't even realize she'd bared her fangs. "See something you like?"

Her eyes snapped to his, and she smiled toothily at him. "Yes."

He advanced upon her. As he did, his cock thickened. He paused in front of her. "Do you want more?"

She smiled. "Yes." She encircled his cock in her hand and leaned forward to flick her tongue over the pulsating head. He sighed deeply and braced his hands on her shoulders. She drew the length of him into her mouth. He groaned and leaned his head back. His hands clenched on her shoulders as she sucked him in and out of her mouth. She cupped his balls in one hand and stroked him with the other. Her teeth dragged softly across his firm shaft.

"I want you again," he said in a rasp. "Now."

She ignored him. She rolled his balls in her hand, and he growled low in his throat. He gripped the back of her head and pushed more deeply into her mouth. She stroked her hand swiftly up and down his shaft as she sucked him. She felt his cock jump and pulse in her mouth. Her mouth turned up slightly.

He groaned and tightened his fingers in her hair. His body tensed. "Don't stop. I'm going to come."

She didn't stop. She squeezed his balls and swirled her tongue on the moist head of his cock. She felt him pulse inside the cool depths of her mouth. He shouted out as his hot, salty seed pumped into her mouth. He didn't let her move away for a moment. He continued to thrust in and out, breathing heavily.

When she pulled away, he opened his eyes and looked down at her. He didn't move. She could hear the rapid thump of his heart. His come was salty like his blood. Her eyes lingered on the vein in his throat. "Bronwyn." Her eyes snapped back to his face. He tilted his head. "Do it."

She didn't hesitate. She was upon him in seconds, biting into the vein in his throat and sucking the hot, thick blood into her mouth. His hands convulsed on her hips. He moaned. He fumbled at her waistband and shoved his hand beneath her panties to rub frantically at her clit as she fed upon him.

She moaned. His blood was like an aphrodisiac. His ministrations coaxed an effortless orgasm from her. She clung onto him, riding out the pleasure as his blood dripped from her mouth to his bare shoulders. She felt him stiffen suddenly. His hands slowed their movements. If she took more from him, she would weaken him. She jerked her head away abruptly.

His eyes drooped slightly, and he dropped down onto the bed. A curl of concern thrummed though her. "Are you all right?" she asked a little hesitantly. "Did I take too much?"

He glanced down at his cock. Despite her attention, it was still hard and hot. "I'm so turned on right now."

She laughed. "So am I, but we have to work."

He sighed and nodded. "Yeah." He gripped her hips to wrap his arms around her waist. She bent down to kiss him. He suckled her tongue. She sighed and pulled away. "If we don't stop now, we'll be here all day."

"I'm okay with that." He tugged the top of her tank top down to expose her left breast. He licked her nipple. He gripped her bottom and dragged her against him.

She moved so quickly, she was across the room before he realized she'd pulled away. He sighed. "Get dressed, Remy."

He smiled. "You mind if I take a quick shower first? A cold one."

She waved her hand. She adjusted her clothes and perched on the edge of the bed to wait for him. When he emerged a few minutes later, his hair was wet around his blue eyes, but he was dressed in jeans and a white tee-shirt. He looked composed, but she could still smell the blood and arousal on him. She could smell her own come on him, despite his shower.

She took a hitching breath and rose to stride from the room before she tossed him back down on the bed and took her fill of his blood and his sex. Her quim pulsed. She didn't think he could survive the full force of her passion, despite the dark energy that super-charged his body.

Fallon, Skye and Noah were already in the lab when they entered. Dawn had risen, and the vampire Gregor must have been tucked up somewhere light tight to wait out the day. Bronwyn didn't miss this. She didn't miss being a slave to the changing day or the rising of the sun. If Remy's coworkers noticed the evidence of her time with him, they didn't respond as the vampire had. They looked up at them.

"You're looking well, Bronwyn," Skye remarked impassively.

She inclined her head and sat in the chair Remy rolled toward her. "I'm fine. I have survived worse attacks." She glanced at Noah. "You did not catch him."

He scowled. "No. It led us through a few streets, but it got away before we could figure out where it was going."

"Bronwyn had an idea," Remy said.

They all looked at her. She lifted an eyebrow. "The demons. How is our scientist getting him?"

Skye shook his head. "There's no way to know. There are a number of black market demon trades."

"Yes, but what if he is opening little rifts all over the place?"

"Snatching them out to experiment on them?" Noah said. "That would be horrifying."

"Just like everything else he is doing," Remy added.

Skye considered this. "Yes. He could be doing that."

Fallon's cell phone trilled through the laboratory. She looked down at it. "It's Anna Fisk." She waved her hand excitedly to hush them as she answered. "Fallon Weir." She paused a moment to listen. "Yes…Yes…No, he isn't in trouble. We just have a few questions to ask him about his work with the Secret Service… Yes." Her fingers moved on the virtual keyboard as she listened to Anna Fisk on the other end of the line. "Uh, huh…Right. Okay…Thank you." She didn't turn to them as she hung up her phone. "He's not in San Francisco. He's been living in Maine since he left the Agency."

"Did you get a number?" Remy asked, sitting down in the chair beside Bronwyn.

"Yes. I'm dialing it now. I'll put it on speaker."

Dr. Ambrose Fisk was already expecting her call. He picked up on the second ring. "Hello?"

"Dr. Fisk, this is Fallon Weir with the Secret Service Paranormal Sector. You were expecting my call?"

"Yes, Agent Weir. I understand you're looking for a biochemist."

"So to speak. There have been some reports of unusual creatures in the Bay Area. Creatures who display characteristics of multiple creatures simultaneously."

Dr. Fisk was silent for a moment. When he spoke, his voice was grim. "You mean hybrid creatures."

"Yes. Something like that."

"I was afraid when Anna told me you called that was what you were looking for."

Fallon frowned. "What do you mean? Have you heard of something like this before?"

"Yes."

"When?"

"When I worked for the Agency. A lab assistant of mine, Dr. Thierry Ashby, was interested in that sort of thing." Fallon's fingers flew over her keyboard at his words. "He posited that it was possible to create creatures like roses on trees."

"I'm sorry?"

"It is possible to splice a rose vine to a tree, creating a new plant that is both rose and tree. A single rose stem will grow out of a tree trunk if it is placed just right under the right conditions."

"Could you do it with creatures?"

"I've never seen it done, but I saw his notes on the subject. I believe it's possible with the right creatures under the right circumstances."

"Did he do it?"

"I don't know. His theories and experiments were outlandish and inappropriate."

"Such as?"

Dr. Fisk hesitated a moment. "My responsibility with the Agency was to study the creatures we captured, test their blood, body fluids and cells to determine if there is some gene responsible for lycanthropy, the genetic structures of demons, how physiology changes when humans turn to vampires. Thierry was more interested in how the creatures reacted to stress and other conditions. He wanted to see how long it took a vampire's arm to grow back, if a were's arm would grow back and so forth. He was injuring the creatures, which was not the purpose of our lab. We were interested in preventing the genes, manufacturing a vaccine, if you will."

"For lycanthropy?"

"Yes. There is nothing that could prevent a human being turned by a vampire if the vampire is quite determined."

"What about demons?" Skye asked. "Did you have any?"

"Yes, but they all had varying physiology, different characteristics and abilities."

"Right."

"When I discovered his experiments, I discharged him from his duties."

"Have you heard of or from Dr. Ashby since then?"

"No. I have not attempted to keep tabs on him. He and I were not friends. He was assigned to me by the Agency, and once I let him go, I was glad to see the back of him. He gave me the creeps."

"Did he have any dealings with magic? Anything to do with it?" Skye asked.

146

"He was interested in the subject. He would often read magical texts while on break, but he was a biologist foremost. I understand magic exists, working for the Agency, but I prefer not to consider it in my work."

"But he did?"

"Perhaps. He definitely might have."

"Is there anything else you know about him that might help us find him?"

Dr. Fisk sighed. "No. He did not talk about any family or friends. He kept to himself. It seemed to me as though his work was his life. There was nothing else for him, as far as I knew."

"All right. We appreciate your time, Dr. Fisk. We will contact you if there is anything else we require."

Dr. Fisk did not sound enthusiastic about this as he hung up. Fallon spun in her chair to face the others. "Well, at least we finally have a lead."

"What did you discover about him?" Skye asked.

She'd already pulled up Dr. Thierry Ashby's files as they'd spoken to his former employer. "There isn't much about him. He was educated at MIT. He's been on a few research projects, but he's never led one. He joined the Agency about five years ago. He was let go last year due to inappropriate use of government property and misconduct against a test subject."

"That's just creepy," Noah muttered.

"Where is he now?" Bronwyn demanded.

"He dropped off the radar after he left the Secret Service." She paused. "No, there's something here."

"What is it?"

"He was arrested on suspicion of murder in Chicago."

"Murder?"

"Yeah. Let me see if I can pull up the file." Her fingers moved so rapidly, even Bronwyn could barely keep up. She was inside the arrest records in seconds. "It looks like the murder of a young woman. Her body was found out back near a warehouse he was renting. He was released due to lack of evidence."

"Was the murder ever solved?" Remy asked.

"No, but they didn't have enough to bring against him at trial."

"What do we know about the woman?" Skye asked.

"Her name was Daphne Evans. She was just a regular woman, by all accounts. She was a photographer, didn't have any family. She was reported missing by her assistant."

"Ah."

"What is it?"

"She was a werewolf."

"How do you know?" Bronwyn asked.

Skye pushed his glasses up on his nose. "She's in our database. She was part of a wolf-pack in Chicago we investigated several years ago."

"So she might have been one of the earlier victims," Remy mused. "He disposed of her when the experiments failed."

"Maybe."

"So, it sounds like he's our guy," Noah put in keenly. He seemed happy to finally have something to latch on to.

"Yes, it sounds as if he is."

"What about the property records around here?" Remy asked. "Anything attached to Ashby's name?"

Fallon sounded shocked. "Actually, yes. He's been renting a storage space in the Castro."

"The Castro? I thought the lab was in the Tenderloin," Noah said, frowning. "Have we been looking in the wrong place?"

"It's possible. This is San Francisco. It isn't exactly a metropolitan. I'm sure the creature could travel that far, as quickly as it moves. Perhaps it prefers the Tenderloin as a hunting ground."

Bronwyn shot to her feet. "Let's go check it out. If we're lucky, we can stop all this before anyone else becomes its prey."

#

The Redi-Store lot in the Castro was quiet. Large, modular metal storage units sat in neat rows inside a tall, electric fence. There was no one nearby, and it seemed almost as if a heavy dark cloud hung over the area. The concrete did not echo with their footsteps. The sounds were muted and almost forlorn.

"This sure looks like the sort of place a mad scientist would experiment on a bunch of monsters," Noah muttered in a subdued voice. He hoisted his gun on his shoulder as though preparing himself for a fight.

"What's the unit number?" Remy demanded.

"315," Fallon replied. Her voice sounded tight and small. She didn't spend much time out in the field. Even in the dreary, dismal gloom of the day, her pale skin was already turning pink.

They strode carefully through the aisles of featureless units. Numbers were stamped on the roll up doors in faded black paint. Bronwyn sniffed the air like a dog scenting its prey in the air. There was a faint, metallic crackle in the air but it didn't smell like vampires or werewolves. It didn't smell strange or confused like the monster that had attacked her. It might have been magic or the terrible, chaotic energy that lingered around the creature that had attacked her.

They followed the numbers to unit 315. It was silent and locked with a large, heavy padlock. Bronwyn stepped past the others toward it. She didn't speak. She couldn't smell anything. She couldn't hear anything inside. Noah lifted his gun and fired at the lock. It didn't break. The bullet ricocheted and struck a nearby unit. Remy and Fallon shouted. Bronwyn spun on Noah with a glare. "Don't do that. This is San Francisco, not the boondocks. You think there aren't bullet proof locks? You might hurt someone."

Noah shrugged sheepishly. "Sorry."

She stepped forward and seized the lock. She snapped it as if it were made of plastic. "Sometimes a little delicacy is in order."

He rolled his eyes and readied his gun. She glanced at the others. They looked braced. She yanked up on the door. It rolled up with a grating sound.

A large, hairy form burst out of the opened door and lunged at Bronwyn. The others shouted in surprise as it knocked her down. Remy darted forward, but she'd already flipped it beneath her. It struggled feebly. Noah stepped forward and pointed his gun at its head. It snapped half-heartedly with its long, sharp fangs and flailed its thick, hairy arms. Its dark eyes darted wildly around at them. There was no intelligence in its gaze. There was only fear.

Bronwyn leapt off it. It was alive, but it had used the last of its strength to pounce on her. She sighed. It didn't get up. It curled up into a fetal position on the concrete at her feet. "It's starving to death." Her voice was low.

"Poor thing," Fallon whispered. "It looks almost human."

There was human flesh between the patches of hair and scales. It turned its head and looked up at Bronwyn. There was such pain and anguish in its eyes, she did not stop to consider what she was doing. She stepped forward and snapped its neck abruptly in her hands.

"Whoa!" Remy and Noah exclaimed together.

"What did you do that for?" Noah demanded, shocked.

She looked up at him with a cold glint in her eyes. "It was suffering horribly. It wanted to die."

"We could have questioned it! It might have been able to tell us what we need to know."

"No. It was no longer intelligent. It was nothing more than a bundle of nerves. Of pain and suffering. There was no humanity or awareness left in it. It was kinder to let it go."

Remy sighed and stood over the creature. "I wonder why Ashby left it here. He doesn't seem like the type to leave evidence. He just left it for dead."

Fallon's eyes were moist as she stared at the monster. "Maybe it escaped like the others and couldn't find its way back to the current lab. Maybe it just came to the last place it knew like an animal."

A chill crept up Bronwyn spine. She spun away from the sad, broken and terrible patchwork monster. "At least now we can study what he's doing to them," Noah muttered.

"And now we know it was Ashby who was responsible."

"Or someone using his name, which is almost good enough." Bronwyn stepped forward into the storage unit. She held up her hand to stop Remy following her. "There's nothing here. No evidence. I can't smell anything. It's clean. I think he wandered here on accident."

"How did he get in? And how did he lock the door after himself?"

She shook her head. "I don't know. Perhaps...Perhaps the lock wasn't there when it came back. Perhaps someone discovered it and locked it in."

"And didn't call anyone?" Fallon asked grimly.

"It's possible," Remy put in. "This isn't exactly a place the renters want the police crawling around."

"That's awful." Fallon's voice was a whisper. "It must have been torture to be locked up like that."

"People are afraid of what they don't understand." Bronwyn spun and lifted the creature in her arms. It smelled metallic like blood and wet dog. It smelled like death, though it had been dead only moments. The smell had been building for days. The creature felt heavy and broken in her arms.

Noah reared back as Bronwyn spun toward him with the creature. She rolled her eyes. "Are you squeamish?"

"I'm not squeamish!"

"Good. I'm taking it back to the lab."

He opened his mouth to reply, but she was gone in a flash. He sighed and looked at Remy. "I'll never get use to vampires."

* * *

Skye bent over the monster on the slab in a cold, starkly lit laboratory in the basement of the Agency headquarters. "This is interesting."

Bronwyn didn't approach the lab table. She leaned against the concrete wall on the opposite side of the room. It felt like a morgue. She felt oddly out of place there. Morgues were for humans. When she died, her undead body would disintegrate into a pile of ash. She would leave nothing behind. "What is?"

"It's just as Dr. Fisk suggested. It appears as though he's cut off the limbs and spliced on new ones. The monster seems to have regenerated and integrated the attached limbs slowly over time. Their DNA's been fundamentally altered into something new and unrecognizable."

"Are they stable?"

He shook his head. "There's no way to tell how long they might have lived in this state. The DNA does not seem to be broken down; it's just mutated. These creatures might die in a matter of days or weeks or live to be hundreds of years old. There's no way to know without observing them in a controlled environment for the duration of their lives."

Remy sighed from the other side of the table. "So the doctor's torturing these creatures. He's harvesting limbs and body parts from other creatures and forcing the monsters to regenerate around the new parts."

"Yes."

Bronwyn shuddered slightly. "Wolves don't regenerate. They heal quickly, but their parts don't grow back over time like vampires."

"I suspect that's why he keeps requiring more subjects from which to harvest the parts. He keeps losing them in the process." He pointed toward the creature's shoulder. Bronwyn didn't move toward him to see what he was indicating. "Here it seems as though he tried a couple different arms. The shoulder meets part of a different body and the new arm has been attached to that."

"Creepy." Fallon muttered from the other side of the room. She was turned toward the wall as though she meant to block the sight of both the creature and Bronwyn. She stared at Remy's back as though she might drill a hole through it.

"That is the most appalling thing I've ever seen," Remy remarked. "I can't believe someone would do this, even for an experiment."

"There are a lot of things people do to each other that are ghastly."

"There are a lot more things they do to us," Bronwyn snapped. "They consider us monsters and assume that we do not have a soul or feelings and cannot understand what's happening to us."

Fallon's shoulders hunched as though she was protecting herself against Bronwyn's words.

"When I find the monster that did this..."

Remy was beside her instantly. He caught her shoulders bracingly. Perhaps he did truly know who she was. He looked at her as though he understood her completely, as though he knew the rage and compassion that flowed through her so intensely, she could hardly contain it. She avoided his gaze. She didn't need him to understand that.

His voice was low and gentle. "Let's let Skye work. We can't do any good here, watching this."

She scowled. "We know what happened and who did it. We just can't find him!"

"I know. But we will."

"We can't just keep letting this go on. He's still got an army of these things as we speak. He could be carving them up right now."

Skye paused and looked up at her. "This isn't the creature that attacked you?"

"No. This one's been starving for days. The one who attacked me was healthy."

"But that means--"

"It means there are more of them. Who knows how many? You were right. There could be dozens." Her voice was harsh.

Remy frowned. "We should focus on the demons. We have to figure out how he's getting them."

"They aren't walking the streets to be taken," Fallon said. "We can see when the rifts open and take them out before they can cause any trouble."

Bronwyn spun on her. "What do you mean you can see when they open? You have a way to monitor that?"

"Of course. This is the government," Skye replied. "We can see any time a rift opens to a demon dimension."

"So have there been any?"

"Not that we know of. We can check the logs."

"Come on," Remy ordered. He took her hand and tugged her toward the door. She didn't resist him. She followed him upstairs to the systems lab. Fallon trailed several paces behind them.

She sat down at her computer and punched up the topographical map. There were several small dots scattered around the city. "What are those dots?" Bronwyn demanded.

Fallon shook her head. "Just some random blips. Magic hot spots. They're not big or long enough to be a rift."

"What do you mean?"

"Dimensional rifts usually have a larger pattern. They aren't so small."

"But what could they be, then? What else does this monitor?"

"Large concentrations of magical energy."

"These weren't large enough to investigate? They were large enough to trip your equipment. Why didn't you look into them?"

Remy frowned. "There isn't anyone monitoring this all day. We've been focused on the creature attacks. I didn't think of watching it or looking into the blips. They happen all the time"

"Well, how about now? Vamps and dogs are still going missing. If he's using demons, too, he must need a steady supply. They regenerate, but not as quickly as vampires." She frowned. "The donors seem to die frequently enough."

"If we can get a real time blip, maybe we can find him."

"I'll monitor the screen," Fallon said in a low voice. "There isn't much else for me to do."

Remy nodded. "Thanks, Fallon." He looked at Bronwyn. "Come on. There's nothing more we can do here. We should get some rest. When we get a blip, we have to be ready to fight."

Bronwyn lifted an eyebrow. His blue eyes glittered. Heat curled in her belly. She didn't argue, and she didn't look back at Fallon, whose breath hitched almost imperceptibly. When they entered his bedroom, Remy did not wait or try to talk to her. He yanked her into his arms and kissed her. He pushed her jacket from her shoulders and tugged her shirt over her head. He squeezed her breasts as she fumbled at his belt, sliding her hands over the firm muscles of his bottom as she pushed his pants down.

He was already hard. He kicked his pants aside and broke the kiss long enough to whip his shirt over his head. He caught her hips and spun her abruptly. She shimmied out of her pants as he pushed them down and kicked them aside as he had done to his. He unfastened her bra and reached around to cup her breasts, rolling the nipples between his fingertips.

Heat rushed through her. He bent her over and nudged her legs apart to thrust abruptly inside her in one swift movement. She moaned and braced herself on the bed. Remy gripped her hips and growled with each hard, rough thrust. He didn't reach down to rub her clit or coax her orgasm gently from her. His cock drove deep and forcefully inside her belly. Tension built up in her belly, and she cried out as it crashed over her.

Remy grunted and came in the same instant. His movements slowed and he panted for several seconds. Then he caught her waist and drew her down to lay beside him on the bed. She smiled as he leaned over her. She lifted her hand to brush her fingertips over his cheekbones.

"You really care about them, don't you?"

She blinked. "What do you mean?" She sounded wary.

154

"The creatures. It's why you do it. You care."

"So?"

"It's unusual for a vampire."

"Not really. The natural traits we possessed in life are magnified when we're vamped. We feel rather well. Rather better than humans, I think." She glanced away. "Many of us hide it. Some think it makes us vulnerable, but I think my feelings make me stronger. Resolute. They keep me going when I see horror like this every day."

He smirked. "It probably helps when you're the biggest, baddest monster."

"Yeah. It sure does."

He leaned down and pressed his mouth to hers. His lips were full and soft. "We'll find Ashby. We'll stop this and make it right."

She nodded. "I know." She was certain. She knew she would find him, and she knew exactly what she would do when she did. They all knew, even Remy. He didn't want to believe it yet, but there was nothing he would be able to do about it when the time came. If he got in her way, he would regret it. At the thought, her stomach sank strangely. She sighed. "I just hope it's soon."

* * *

Noah tipped back in his chair in front of the large, glass monitor. His eyes drooped. His head fell forward onto his chest. Beside him, Fallon stared silently at her computer screen. She didn't snap at Noah or attempt to awaken him. Her expression was dark and sullen. The rest of the world might not have existed at all.

On Noah's screen, a soft, almost inaudible blip appeared on the radar.

Upstairs, Remy and Bronwyn dressed in the clothes they'd hastily discarded. He smiled at her as he paused to watch her tug her tank top over her head. "I could get used to this."

She looked at him. "Well, don't. I'm not going to be around for much longer. Just until we solve this and I stop Ashby."

Remy strode forward and wrapped his arms around her waist. "There's no way to convince you to hang around for a while?"

Bronwyn sighed and glanced away. "Remy, I told you..."

"I know what you told me, but I refuse to accept it." He caught her chin to turn her face to him. "There is something between us, Bronwyn. Give it a chance."

She considered him for a moment. Then she frowned and looked away. She wanted nothing more than she wanted to remain with him, even in San Francisco. There was something between them. She'd had lovers, but Remy St. John was different. He made her feel alive, more alive than she'd felt when she'd actually been alive.

There wasn't room in her life for those feelings. She didn't need them. She didn't want them.

"Come on, Wyn. You could take a vacation from the killing and hunting and avenging angel bit."

She sighed. "I don't think I can, Remy."

"Why?"

"This is why I choose to do this. Those creatures. To hunt evil, to stop things like this from happening. I can't just stop doing it."

"You've helped people. You've earned the right to relax for a little while. You deserve to have a life."

"I lost that when I gave up my human life."

"No. Bronwyn, you didn't. Vampires can have lives, too." He smiled slightly. "Don't be so dramatic. It's your calling, apparently, but it doesn't have to be your whole life."

She pushed him away. "Who are you to tell me what to do with my life? I make my own choices. I won't let a man tell me what to do."

He caught her around the waist and drew her back against him. "That's not what I meant. It's not what I mean to do. I just want to be with you."

She shook her head and stepped out of his arms. "I can't talk about this right now, Remy. We have something we need to be doing. Let's just finish the job, and we can talk about it then."

He frowned. "You'll talk about it then?"

"Yes." She avoided his gaze.

"Promise me."

She rolled her eyes. "Fine. I promise."

"Okay." He didn't sound convinced. That was all right. She didn't mean it anyway. It did quiet him down, anyway. She could figure out what to do about him later. Right now, her rage and bloodlust pulsed through her.

Fallon didn't turn to look at them as they entered. Noah didn't seem to notice them at all. His head lolled back. Bronwyn's head snapped to the monitor above his kicked up feet. She could hear a tiny, almost silent blip.

"There." She rushed forward so quickly, Noah started and nearly toppled backward in his chair. She caught the back of his chair to steady him.

"What? What is it?" he asked sleepily.

She frowned at him. "There's a blip."

He squinted at the screen. "You're right. It's small. Right there in the Tenderloin."

She rolled her eyes. "Can you pinpoint it?"

"Yeah." He punched up the coordinates. Beside him, Fallon plugged them into her computer.

"It's a warehouse," Fallon announced.

Bronwyn spun toward Remy. "Let's go."

He stepped in front of her. "Wait, we--"

"No. I'm going now."

She was out of the room like a flash of lightning. Remy chased after her. "Wyn, wait! I'm coming with you!

She paused in the lobby. Gregor was beside her instantly. He looked as though he'd just awakened. He must have heard their shouts from his room. "Is it time? Have we found him?"

Bronwyn nodded. "I'm going now."

"You need backup. We're coming with you."

She sighed, but she suspected they would come whether she wanted them to or not. "All right."

They didn't keep her waiting long. Noah and Remy hurtled down the stairs, loaded with weapons. Remy nodded at her. "Let's go."

The city raced past, but not quickly enough. Bronwyn vibrated beside Remy in the passenger seat. Gregor and Noah were silent and tense. Remy didn't glance from the road as he sped through the streets. "We need a plan."

"We go inside and we kill him," Bronwyn hissed.

"That isn't a plan."

"I don't like plans."

"We have no idea what we're going to find when we get there," Gregor put in tightly.

"I like Bronwyn's plan," Noah added.

"We can't just go in half-cocked. If he has an army of those creatures, we'll be outnumbered."

She sighed. He wasn't wrong. She had already experienced the monsters' power. "We don't have a choice. If we want to stop this, we have to go in."

Remy scowled. "All right. We'll check it out. If it looks safe to enter, we'll go in."

She glanced at him, but she didn't reply to this. She suspected he knew what she was thinking. She was going in anyway.

When Remy pulled to a stop in front of the address Fallon had given them, she was out of the SUV faster than any of them could move. She paused outside. It was grey and featureless. It was surrounded on both sides by similar structures, but it seemed as though the blip's location was suspended somehow in space and time, as though the buildings around it were alive. It was dead. No one was around. There was no sound, despite the earliness of the evening hour. The sound seemed to disappear into the air around the warehouse, as if it were a black hole or a vacuum.

She stared around her with a furrow in her brow. Her voice was muted and subdued. "I can feel the magic in the air. It's metallic, like a lightning strike, but something is shielding it from me."

"And our instruments," Remy added, pausing beside her with a scowl.

"How?" Gregor demanded.

"I don't know," Bronwyn said. "It must be some kind of spell."

"He's in there," Noah growled. "He's opening a rift right now."

Gregor glanced at Bronwyn. He seemed to have the same idea as her, despite Remy's caution. "Should we go in? We could stop him before he can draw out another demon."

"We need a plan," Remy barked. "He has a patchwork army in there."

158

"Yes. He does." Bronwyn cut a glance at Noah. "You've got a big gun, don't you?"

He squared his shoulders. "Yeah. Big enough. This time I'm prepared." He hoisted a large cannon on his shoulder.

Another black SUV screeched to a halt on the street behind them. They spun toward it. Noah raised his cannon, but he lowered it as Skye stepped out of the vehicle. He wore black from head to toe, and he shouldered a cannon even larger than Noah's. He smirked at them. "Fallon told me what you were up to. She thought I might like in on it."

They stared at him. "You haven't been out in the field for years," Gregor remarked.

He shrugged. "I think I've still got it. And I brought guns for everyone."

Bronwyn smirked as Remy ducked into the trunk to hoist his own gun on his shoulder. Fallon stepped out of the passenger side. She had a gun strapped to her back. She looked almost rosy. She lifted her chin. "You guys are going to need more help if you want to take this guy on. I've seen him. He's nuts."

Bronwyn eyed them. "I don't need a gun, but I think that should be enough."

"Are we going to do this or just stand around admiring each other's guns?" Skye asked.

She didn't need to be told twice. She strode around the side of the warehouse. There was a large, unmarked grey metal door. There was no lock, but there was a keypad on the left side. She ignored it. She kicked in the door. It flew off its hinges. Gregor grabbed Noah out of the way just in time.

The warehouse was empty. No man or monster was inside. There weren't any boxes or equipment or furniture. It looked as though no one had used the huge, high-ceiled concrete space for a very long time. Bronwyn's nerves sang. The others seemed tense and poised for attack.

She felt something. Something was wrong. This warehouse was not what it seemed.

Remy flew backward suddenly as though something had knocked into him. Bronwyn spun. "Remy!" He flailed and struggled against the invisible attacker. She pounced. She could feel the creature, but she could not see it. She could feel hair, scales and ice cold skin beneath her fingers. She cursed and dragged it bodily from Remy. Thick gashes opened on his cheeks and throat, but he scrambled away.

"Get out of the way, Wyn!" He aimed his weapon and fired it at the invisible creature in her arms. She felt it jerk. She heard it yelp.

"They're here!" she shouted. "We just can't see them! Something is shielding them."

They didn't need her to tell him. They were already fighting off the invisible creatures, firing their guns as if into the thin air. Blood spattered the floor, but there were no bodies or creatures. Gashes and teeth marks appeared on their skin. Bronwyn cursed. "We need to bring down the shield!" Remy growled. "We're going to hit each other."

Skye fired his weapon. A loud, anguished howl rose up in the strangely silent melee. He stepped back and lifted a hand. He chanted in a low, strange language. Large, deep scratches appeared on his cheeks and neck. He gritted his teeth and continued to chant. Bronwyn raced to his side, fighting off the claws and teeth that snapped around him. She couldn't see the creatures, couldn't smell them or sense them. Pain lanced across her belly as claws tore into it.

She kept fighting. They all kept fighting. Behind them, someone laughed. Bullets showered the empty space from which it came as they all fired in the direction of the sound. Glass shattered.

Suddenly, everything came into focus.

They all paused in shock. Patchwork creatures lay around their feet, twitching and moaning in pain. They were inside a large, concrete laboratory. Small, glass walled cells around the room held vampires, werewolves and strange, inhuman creatures with red, yellow or blue skin, horns, scales and mouths of teeth like sharks. The creatures were docile, as if they'd been drugged. Some of them were missing arms or legs. Others had large patches of skin removed from their chests or faces. In one corner, a pile of discarded body parts were piled up as if they'd been tossed haphazardly aside. They stank of rot and death.

Thierry Ashby stood in the center of the room behind a small, wooden podium upon which was a large, ancient and crumbling book. Before him was a large, metal lab table. There was no monster upon the table, but there was dried blood. Thick, leather straps hung off the side. Bloody knives, scalpels and saws sat in a careless heap upon the table beside it.

The doctor was a tall, gaunt man in a bloody lab coat. His large, dark eyes stood out against his starkly pale skin. He might have been handsome once before he'd gone crazy. His features were even and rich. Now his eyes glowed with a mad, furious light. His hair was wild and curly. It looked as if he hadn't combed or washed it in several days. It was dark and dirty. Black, ugly energy swirled almost tangibly in the air in front of him. No demons came through the small, churning hole in the veil between their worlds. They'd interrupted him.

Behind Ashby, a large, pale white creature with large, flat scales upon its serpentine body lay amidst a shower of shattered glass. Thick, ruby red blood poured over its tail. It was still twitching slightly, but the expression on its humanoid face was almost peaceful. Skye pointed toward it. "A Solomos demon. They have the ability to deprive the senses. It must have what's been shielding the lab."

"And one of you killed it," Bronwyn said in a low voice.

"That is truly a shame. They are a very peaceful race."

She looked at him incredulously. "A peaceful demon?"

"Not all of them want to run rampant and destroy humanity. Some of them are actually quite gentle."

"Can we save the lecture for when we're not in the middle of a battle?" Remy snapped.

"Right." They all spun as one and aimed their guns around at the three patchwork creatures looming around Dr. Ashby like watch dogs. Bronwyn ignored the creatures and turned an expression of such searing, murderous hatred upon Ashby, a normal man would have begged for his life. This doctor was insane. He didn't seem to understand or regard his danger at all. He was still laughing, but there was no humor in his eyes. There was nothing in his eyes but a mad, glittering light.

"Destroy them." Ashby's voice was a high-pitched roar.

The patchwork monsters moved as one toward Bronwyn and the agents. They were large, and mad energy hung in the air around them. Bronwyn could smell them now. There was a strange, metallic smell around them like blood and lightning. They all had humanoid features beneath the matte of hair and patches of shiny, glowing scales and marble pale skin. They were larger than normal men, as though Ashby had selected the largest and strongest of the creatures to bond together. Their eyes were wild and furious as though they were fighting to obey their master, resisting the compulsion to flee or turn upon the doctor.

Bronwyn's eyes snapped to them. "He did this to you." Her voice was low and mesmerizing. The stopped their approach as if suspended for a moment in indecision. The agents remained poised for attack, but they went motionless. "He made you these things. Part vamp, part wolf, part demon. What were you

161

before, in your heads before he carved you up and struck the wrong body parts on you?"

"I made them better!" Ashby hissed. "I made them masterpieces. The ultimate creatures."

"You made them monsters!"

Ashby lifted a hand and pointed a finger at her. His eyes flashed. "They were already monsters."

"That is no excuse for what you did to them. You do not have the right to play god, to do these things to creatures."

He lifted his chin. Her hypnotic voice and eyes seemed to have no affect on him. "I have the power. I have the knowledge. That gives me the right. They are my children. My creations. They will protect me."

"No." Bronwyn's lips turned up slightly at the corners. "They will not."

Ashby scowled. "Destroy them!"

The creatures snapped out of their trance. They rushed suddenly toward the agents who waited with their cannons poised to fire. The creatures did not seem intent on attack. They did not strike or bare their teeth as they stampeded Skye's team. They did not attempt to dodge the sudden barrage of gunfire. Their eyes looked almost intelligent, almost alive as they bounded determinedly into the spray of bullets.

The agents did not stop firing until the creatures lay upon the floor at their feet. Blood spattered the floor and walls around them, splattered their clothes and the patchwork monsters. The creatures did not stir. They made a sound; a single, collective noise that sounded almost like a gentle, relieved sigh. The strange, anguished sound lanced through Bronwyn's chest like a knife. She spun on Dr. Ashby.

"Your army is dead."

He looked wild for a moment. His head bobbled as though he were looking for his protectors or a way to escape the agents and vampire in front of him. He threw out his hand toward them and tossed his head back and forth. "No!"

Remy stepped forward. "We have to take you in, Ashby. It's over. You know it is." His tone was so even and almost soothing, Bronwyn's eyes snapped to him. She felt the briefest twinge of admiration for him. She did not regret what she intended to do, but she did regret what it would mean for them.

"Why did the monsters do that?" Fallon whispered, shouldering her cannon and bending down to peer at the bloody fallen creatures.

"They sacrificed themselves," Bronwyn told her without turning around. "They had some intelligence left. They knew what he'd done to them. And they didn't want to be these things anymore."

"He won't be able to do this again." She didn't look at Remy. She didn't like the tone of his voice, the subtle plea that seemed to understand exactly what she intended to do.

It didn't matter. "No. He won't." Bronwyn moved so fast, Remy was blown backward as she passed him to get to the doctor. A long, thin blade shot out from under the sleeve of her leather jacket. She lifted it to the doctor's throat.

Ashby squealed. She glared into his eyes. Remy darted forward and caught Bronwyn's arm. "Wyn, no. Don't kill him."

She cut a disgusted glance in his direction. "He should be punished for what he's done."

"He will. He will be imprisoned for a long time. He won't be able to do it again."

"It's not good enough! Look what he did to all these creatures. Look at the dead and mutilated. Only death is a suitable punishment for him."

"That is not how we do things," Skye growled.

Bronwyn didn't even glance at him. "I don't care how you do things. I am not an agent. I don't work for you."

"Wyn, please," Remy murmured. "I can't let you."

"You don't have any control over what I do."

"Bronwyn! If you do this, I can't save you."

"I don't need you to save me. I can take care of myself."

He stepped forward. He ignored her flash of fang. He ignored the doctor trembling in Bronwyn's arms. "I need you. Don't do this."

She met his glittering blue gaze. She hesitated for the briefest second. It would be easy to fall into the depths of his eyes. It would be so easy to take what he offered, to live a life with him, to stay with him until his human body aged and withered and eventually died. She would enjoy him until that happened. For a moment, she wanted nothing more than to be with him as long as he remained in this life.

Bronwyn glanced back at Ashby. His eyes were wild and panicked. He struggled against her hold, but she ignored him. His life belonged to her now. She could do with it as she pleased. She swiveled her head to look at Remy's agents behind her. They looked uncertain, as if they could not decide whether or not to stop or shoot her. They wouldn't shoot her. They wouldn't do anything. They meant nothing to her.

She did not meet Remy's gaze again. She pressed the knife against Ashby's throat. He squeaked.

"Stop her!" Fallon cried. "She's going to kill him!"

It was too late. It was already done. Bronwyn pulled the bloody knife from Ashby's throat and stepped away from him. He slumped to the ground. His eyes were still open in surprise, but there was no mad, gleaming life left in them. She turned away from the body and looked at Remy.

His expression stopped her in her tracks. He didn't look angry. Instead, he looked so heartbroken, a curl of pain lanced through her chest. A single tear streaked down her cheek. She didn't bother to wipe it away.

In the blink of an eye, she was gone, and the agents were left alone among the dead and the dying.

CHAPTER EIGHT

It was over. The patchwork monsters were gone. Their depraved creator was finished. The few unfortunate test subjects that had survived the raid were languishing in an Agency infirm facility outside of town. They would live, but they would never be the same. They would never shake the horror they'd witnessed and experienced at the deranged doctor's hands.

But it was over. At least until the next mad scientist or wicked sorcerer.

Remy stared out the window. It was raining. He watched the fog swirl around the streets and on top of the tall, muted buildings outside. He felt empty and lost. There was nothing for him out there. He wasn't sure how it had happened so quickly or even exactly what it was, but he felt as though something had been ripped from him, something that would have given his life meaning for the first time since he'd been ousted from his home.

She was a vampire. He was a human. It would never have worked. It didn't seem to make a difference how emphatically he reminded himself of this.

He spun away from the window and strode downstairs to the lobby. His partners sat in the soft, padded armchairs around the room, sipping coffee. They looked almost relaxed. They looked up at him as he entered with careful expressions, as if they weren't sure how to address him. They had been looking at him this way for days. They spoke to him in hushed voices as if they were at a funeral or beside his death bed.

He wondered if he looked so bad. He'd never felt this bad before, not since the *Castus Vox* had shamed and expelled him. It felt as though the monsters had reached in and ripped out his heart. He had never felt like that about a woman before. He'd never cared if they disappeared from his life. There were always more. None of them were so like him, so driven and righteous. None of them wanted what he wanted, none of the made him feel as though the chaotic world suddenly made sense, as though he would be all right despite his rising madness. Bronwyn had, but then she'd left, and he felt as though the world was spiraling out of control again.

He sighed. The others glanced at each other uncertainly. Skye rose. "I submitted my report on the Ashby incident."

Remy nodded shortly. "What's next, then? Do we hunt down Bronwyn? Bring her in?"

Skye shook his head. He placed a hand on Remy's shoulder. "I stated in the report that Ashby's death was an accident. He died in a struggle."

Remy blinked at him in surprise. "The bastard deserved to die," Gregor hissed. "What he was doing was horrible."

"She killed a man!" Fallon said hotly. "In cold blood. There is no excuse for murder."

"Not even when the world is better off without the victim in it?" Noah asked gently.

"Vigilante justice is not acceptable. We cannot just allow vampires to run around and kill people as they please. That is what we do. It's what the Agency is for. We stop people and creatures from killing as they please. Isn't that why we were created? To bring people like Ashby to justice, not allow him to be slaughtered by a vigilante. To stop vampires like her."

Skye sighed. "I don't think we'll ever agree on the topic, but it's done. Let it go. Ashby has been stopped." He glanced at Remy. "Bronwyn is free to do as she wishes. For now." His eyes glinted suddenly with a cold determination. "But if she ever crosses me again, I will put her on the Agency's most wanted list. We might not be able to stop her or get to her, but we can make life in the U.S. very difficult for her."

Remy laughed. "I don't think she cares much about that. I think she will pretty much do what she wants no matter what." He clapped Skye on the shoulder. "Thanks, Skye."

Skye nodded. "Well. I have a scene clean up to supervise. We still have the piles of bodies to sort through and the casualties to tally."

"Has anyone found Odo yet?"

Gregor rolled his eyes. "He's not among the victims. He was holed up with a nest of vamps in Bulgaria. He suspected it was us who were snatching the vamps off the streets. He was afraid he was next and took off."

Remy scoffed. "Why would we target Odo? He was one of our assets."

"Yeah, well, apparently he got himself into some trouble with a couple tourists. They didn't exactly realize he wasn't just another sparkly vamp knock-off. They reported an attack. He thought we would hunt him."

"Great. And we lose another asset. He was good, too. Where is he now?"

"We can't touch him overseas. I don't think he'll be coming back anytime soon. At least the tourists are taken care of; we got some of our people to clean their heads. They'll return home to Indiana with a few pleasant memories of the Golden Gate Bridge."

"Right. Well, I'm just relieved this is over." Skye sighed. "I haven't seen a bloodbath like this since—well. Since we picked you up, Remy."

Remy scowled and avoided their eyes.

Skye spun away. He was already half-way to the stairs when he added, "You lot monitor the papers and the screens a little more closely for a while, huh? Get to work. This isn't a mini-break."

"Right." They jumped to their feet and trudged toward the systems lab. Remy didn't follow them. He climbed the stairs toward his room slowly. He wasn't ready for another job, more victims and monsters to battle. He just wanted to sleep. He wanted to forget what had happened for a few hours or even a few minutes. His energy felt wild and erratic. Whatever Bronwyn had done while he'd been inside her had contained it for a time, but it wouldn't remain under control forever. He needed to rest.

He moved toward his bed. He didn't feel tired. He felt bone-weary. He doubted he could sleep. He hadn't slept in days.

A shadow moved past his window. He looked up.

Bronwyn was inside before he even sensed her. Her long, dark red hair was damp from the rain outside. Remy didn't say anything to her. He rushed toward her. She met him halfway, crashing her lips into his. He sucked her tongue into his mouth and spun her around toward the bed. They tore at each other's clothes, tossing them aside in a rush to be closer, to press skin against skin.

He lifted her so his throbbing cock rubbed against the moist heat of her quim. He dropped her down on the bed. She opened her legs to him and held out her arms. He did not tease her or keep her waiting. He climbed atop her and guided his cock to her tight, quivering slit. She gasped as he pushed inside. She gripped his bottom to draw him deeper inside and tilted her hips up to meet his thrusts.

Remy stared down into her eyes. They were dark and sparkling. She lifted her head to kiss him. He hooked his arms under her knees to angle her hips up. She moaned against his mouth as he plunged hard into her tight depths. He kneaded her breasts, pinching the nipples between his fingertips. She tore her mouth from his and tossed her head back as her quim tightened around his cock. She moaned as her orgasm exploded around him.

He bent his head into her neck and growled as he pushed frantically toward his climax. She met his thrusts, clinging to him as his movements grew faster and erratic. When he came, he bit down on the soft flesh between her neck and shoulders. He lifted his head to look down at her. He didn't pull out of her. He rolled on his side and drew her up against him.

"You came back."

She rested her chin on his chest and looked up at him. He couldn't read the expression on her face. "Yes."

"Where have you been?"

She sighed. "Cleaning up the mess. Identifying the losses on our side. Letting my people know it's safe to be on the streets again."

"Does this mean you're thinking of staying?"

She ignored the question. "I thought I would be on the Agency's most wanted list by now. I thought I would have to be on the run until they forget about me." She lifted an eyebrow. "You can't be with someone on the run from your own Agency. You should probably be staking me right now."

"I prefer to poke you with other things."

"That is not a good joke."

"I didn't have a lot of time to prepare. Skye reported Ashby's death as an accident on the official record. You're off the hook."

She frowned. "Why would he do that? I thought that's what you guys did--stop people like me doing things like that."

He shrugged. "Most of us agreed he deserved to die. They think you did the right thing."

She didn't look as if this was good news. "I did the right thing. I just didn't follow your rules."

Remy stared at her a long moment. He brushed her long hair behind her shoulders. His hand lingered on her cheek, stroking it gently with his fingertips. She trailed her hand over his bare, muscular chest. He caught her hand. "You can't use the Agency as an excuse to blow me off, Wyn."

She sighed. He was starting to understand her a little more than she liked. "Remy, I'm not the settling down type. I'm not the type to stay in one place. You're bound here."

"Not forever. Five years. What's five years to a vampire?"

She sighed. "Remy..."

"You're telling me you don't feel this way, too?"

She considered it for a long moment. She didn't reply.

"You feel something for me. I know you do."

"Yes." She sighed. "I feel something."

"Just not enough to stay?"

"No. Not enough to stay."

Her words lanced through him. His hands tightened reflexively on her flesh. They left bruises in the shape of his fingertips. The bruises healed instantly.

She lifted her head and looked down at him. There was a dark look in her eye. His stomach sank. He could sense her fear. He understood her better than she was willing to admit. She wanted him. She wanted to stay by his side, but it simply couldn't be. He was a mortal. She was a vampire. He took a hitching breath. And his dark energy would take him one day, strip him of his senses and his sanity. She would have to watch him slip away.

She lifted a hand to brush his dark blonde hair from his gleaming blue eyes. She leaned up and kissed him softly, gently on the mouth. "But enough to come back."

He smiled. She snuggled against his side. He turned his head to rest his cheek upon her dark red hair. He sighed deeply. "Do you have to leave right now?"

"Soon."

"Where are you going?"

She hesitated. He looked down at her. "Ireland."

He lifted an eyebrow. "Why?"

"There is work for me there."

"What sort of work?"

She stared at him. She did not reply to this.

"For Cicely?"

She didn't bristle, but he sensed she was not comfortable with the subject of her sorceress friend. He was surprised when she said, "Yes. She has called for me. I do not know yet for what she needs me."

He nodded. "I will wait for you."

She met his gaze. "Don't."

"Why not?"

"I don't know how long it'll be, Remy. It could be months or years."

"Years?" His voice was low.

"Cicely and I don't age. Sometimes we lose track of time."

He chuckled. "Do you have a cell phone?"

"You want my phone number?"

"I think it's appropriate in this stage of the relationship."

"This isn't a relationship."

"Don't fool yourself, Wyn. This is something much more than that."

She smiled slightly. "All right. Yes, I have a cell phone. I don't receive calls on a subconscious wavelength."

Remy laughed. "I suppose I half-expected you would."

"I have an email, too. I even check it. I'm a very modern girl. I had one of the first computers when they were invented in the twenties."

"The twenties? I don't think that's right."

"Human history is very subjective." She lifted her head to kiss him. "You should get some sleep. You look like you could use it."

He frowned. "I haven't slept in days."

She sighed. "I'm sorry for that."

"Don't be so conceited. I wasn't mooning over you the whole time."

She lifted a skeptical eyebrow, but she didn't say anything to this. She kissed his forehead and settled against him. Her fingertips fluttered with moth's wing softness over his chest and abdomen. Remy closed his eyes. He was asleep in seconds. It was the first time he'd slept since she'd disappeared.

Bronwyn sighed contentedly and rested against him for several long moments. She could hear his heart pounding in his chest. It was strong and rhythmic. His body was powerful, but she could feel the dark artifact's energy pulsating beneath his skin, in his aura. It wouldn't be long before it took him over completely. His blood tasted of power and madness. She watched it pump through his veins beneath his skin. She wanted it. She wanted him.

She slipped carefully from his arms. He didn't seem to notice. He didn't stir. She leaned down and kissed him softly on his full, sensual mouth. She paused at the windowsill and turned back to peer at him one last time.

"Good bye, Remy."

When Remy awoke, she was gone. He shot up into a sitting position. Her side of the bed felt cold and barren. He dropped his head in his hands. He sighed deeply. She wouldn't be back, not for a while, anyway. He looked down at her pillow. A strip of paper lay upon it. There was one long word scrawled across the paper in an elegant, old-fashioned cursive script.

brownynliddle@vampchronlive.com

* * *

"You didn't have a choice."

Bronwyn glanced at Merek through the shadows of the dark, silent courtyard behind the Agency headquarters. "I know."

"He is a human, and he is damaged."

"I know."

Merek looked at her. "You can't stay here. You have work to do in Ireland. Cicely has called for you."

"I know, Merek."

He turned toward her. "You've avenged Linus and the others."

"I have."

"Then why are you still here?"

She looked up at the glow above their heads. The dark curtain hid him from her, but she could sense him there before she saw him. A shadow passed across the window as though he were pacing swiftly from one side of the room to the other. "I don't know."

"Will you stay?"

"No."

"But you will come back."

Bronwyn considered. "I will find my way back here eventually."

"You cannot ignore Cicely for much longer."

She rolled her eyes. "I am leaving tonight."

"Thank you for what you have done for our people here."

She smirked. "But you'll be happy to see the back of me?"

"I will be happy to see the end of this nightmare once and for all."

Bronwyn laughed. "Merek, I'm beginning to think you don't want me here."

"Your presence here is slightly disrupting to our way of life."

"And here I thought I was doing you a favor. Perhaps next time I will not come so quickly when you call."

Now Merek smirked. He inhaled deeply on his cigarette and puffed out the acrid smoke in a series of tiny rings. He jerked his chin toward the window. Remy paused as if he sensed them there, but he did not peer out into the garden. "Yes, you will."

She was silent for a moment. He braced himself as though he expected her to turn on him. She didn't. She smiled a tiny smile. "It was nice seeing you again, Merek."

"You too, Wyn." He turned toward her and smiled. Then, in a flash, he disappeared into the shadows and was gone.

Bronwyn rose up into the air. The slight, gentle breeze lifted her hair and the ends of her long coat. Inside, Remy paced back and forth along the floor. She could sense his black energy coiled in the pit of his belly. It was under control. For now. He would be all right for a little longer.

She smiled a little sadly. She did not move inside or alert him to her presence at his window.

"I will see you again, Remy. But right now, I have things I need to do."

END

172

ABOUT THE AUTHOR

Delia Cortez is the author of the sizzling Brownyn Liddle Vampire Fables from DC Dreams. A private, soft-spoken and enigmatic lady, she rarely leaves her isolated seaside home before nightfall. She spends her time lingering in the shadows, appreciating the darker side of life, and penning her sexiest fantasies for others to enjoy.

Look for

Stick & Dagger

Bronwyn Liddle Vampire Fables: Book Two

Coming Soon from DC Press

www.diogenesclubpress.com